Dragon Train Rebellion

Book 2
Dragon Train Quest

RJ the Story Guy

High Desert Libris

Albuquerque

High Desert Libris
Albuquerque, NM

Publisher's Note: This is a work of fiction. Names, characters, places, and incidents are a product of the author's imagination. Locales and public names are sometimes used for atmospheric purposes. Any resemblance to actual people, living or dead, or to businesses, companies, events, institutions, or locales is completely coincidental.

Cover Art by Celebril, found at https://celebrilart.com/
Book Design by Paul Murray, found at http://gpmurray.com
Text formatting by RJM Creative Arts

Dragon Train Rebellion/RJ the Story Guy. -- 1st ed.
ISBN 978-1-7334361-8-2

This is for the Patriots in Ukraine, Hong Kong,
And others across the world who
Offer their lives for
The freedom of their people

Thanks to my wife whose support and love
Makes it all possible.

Special Thanks to:
Kathy Waggoner
Joyce Hertzoff
Paul Murray
Lisa Durkin
For their intelligent and insightful
Editing and suggestions
That made this a story I proudly share with readers.

Thanks to:
Celebril and
Paul Murray
For their artistic vision.

CONTENTS

ONE

Practice Session

W e soared so high I forgot myself and reached to touch the clouds—but I felt only wet, cold fog. I expected soft billows of pure white wool that floats around our barn when my Dad and I shear the sheep.

I started to complain about the wet clouds when Skye's voice in my head said, *Hang on, Jaiden.*

The blue dragon rotated to the right and dropped us like a rock. Wind blew so hard into my mouth I nearly inflated like a bloated cow. Far below, the brown desert spread out—a dead garden—as the hot wind rose up to sweep away the cold that penetrated the marrow of my bones. The wind burned as we neared the ground way too fast.

I fought to keep from messing my pants.

"Stop! Skye, what are you doing?" She leveled out. Her wings reached wide, caught the desert air like big blue sheets and brought us to a gentle landing.

"Slam! Are you trying to kill me?"

I struggled to pull my bloodless hands—numb from cold and fear—out from under the strap that held me tight to her body. That strip of leather—left over from the harness that attached her to the rigging back in her days when she towed a train—was the only thing that kept me from becoming a red smear on the hard-brown dirt.

I literally fell on my face and hugged the ground.

I thought you said you were never going to hug the ground after aerial training, she said as I heard a hissing chuckle in the giant blue dragon's throat.

"Yeah, well, you didn't say you were going to dive several hundred feet like you were trying to drive us into the dirt like a gate post! You never did that before!"

Of course, I have. Caerulus had me dive several times during training, so I could learn to fly low enough to burn a platoon of humans without crashing into the ground.

"Why wasn't I invited to those so-called training sessions? And just when were you training?" I stomped right up to her as she bent down, filling my vision with her moon-sized blue face. "I should have been with you to start with," I sputtered. My face burned hot from a mix of fear and anger. How dare she—

Because... she said, gathering patience to calm down the berserk little human getting in her face. *You will NOT fly with me when I am burning human soldiers.* She almost sounded like my cranky old grandmother. *Your mission is to get dropped—gently—on the ground to mingle with your kind and gather information.*

"So why did you nearly scare the turds out of me, now?" I demanded. She looked sheepish, which is something I never thought I would see on a dragon's face. I blurted, "OK, I get it, so I'm sorry. I guess I would rather mess my pants a few times than do something boring like gather information."

There you see, she said. *I thought you might enjoy it this one time. Besides, there might be times when you would be dropped off rather quickly.* She smiled and blinked her huge cooper-flecked eyes at me.

I sighed. It was no use. "I never promised to spy on people. I told you I'm not good at fooling people and pretending I'm something I'm not—"

You did quite well to pose as a conductor when we gained entrance into the Big Barn in Portville to rescue my mate and children. So, what do you propose to do for our cause? You're the one who didn't want to be left out.

She was right. Me and my big mouth.

Right then, Caerulus dropped out of the clouds and landed with a flurry of dust and pieces of cactus flying in all directions. If he wasn't so big and kind of scary, I would have complained about getting stung by cactus needles.

Caerulus, Skye said in a way that sent chills down my back. *What is all this commotion? I am training Jaiden to get used to quick landings in case we—*

Good enough, but I think he needs to start working with a silver dragon, he said without waiting for a response from her. *And, here comes a candidate to train with the boy right now.*

Flying low and fast, a silver dragon the size of a horse zoomed up to us and stuck a landing like an eagle grabbing a fish jumping a waterfall.

Caerulus nodded to the shiny silver and smiled. *This is Trigger, who has been training for months. I think he's ready to have a real human on his back so he can learn to fly as one with his rider.* He turned to me with a stern eye. *What do you think, boy?*

My face grew hot with his second reference to me as a boy. "I'm seventeen. Old enough to start working a plot of my own land and build a small home for a wife... that is, if I wanted a wife. But I'm not a *boy.*" The big dragon's stare intensified. "Not in the way you mean it," I said quickly. "I'll take 'young man,' if you like."

Caerulus' stern face slowly broke into a smile that would have otherwise looked scary. *Of course, you're right. If you're going to be a part of our struggle with the human slave masters, then you'll have to be a man just as our dragon warriors have to be ready to behave as adults, not children. But, first, you have to prove yourself.*

He turned and motioned Trigger to approach us.

As the silver slithered over to me, I shuttered and wondered why it wasn't a good feeling. But I shook it off, so I could concentrate on what I was supposed to do.

Here is your ride, young man, Caerulus said. *And, you,* he said to the silver, *here is your rider. Commence flight!*

Trigger strolled over to me and squatted so I could mount him like a horse. I saw only big spines on his back. I knew that when the smallest dragons, the golds, ride silvers, they fit their front and rear legs between the medium-sized silver's two biggest spines, spread about two feet apart. Then they hang onto those thick spines with their claws. Either silvers don't have much feeling in their spines or the golds had a way of hanging on without hurting the silvers.

"This silver could use a good saddle mounted between these big spines," I said.

Skye sent a warm wave of satisfaction into my head. *You're right. What we need are human craftsmen to make some for us because dragons can't do any handwork but—*

"—because dragons have no hands and you have no humans on your side yet..." As interrupted her, I felt a little bad making a complaint like that. "I guess that's kind of what you want me for? Find some humans to help out. For now, I think I'll just hang on. Maybe even I can come up with something. My dad taught me a little leather craft, so we'll see."

Caerulus nodded his head. *Then, let's get started without further discussion. Remember, you guide the silver by pressing your hands on the sides and top of the silver's neck. But if you're flying fast and changing directions quickly you must hang onto those spines with your hands. So, guide through pressing your knees against the gold's shoulders and belly. To stop, pull back on one of his spines farther up his neck.*

"Got it," I said quickly before he continued to state the obvious to me. He must think I was not paying one bit of attention during my training the last several days.

I mounted the silver who shuffled nervously, his body trembling with what I thought was excitement. But it turned out the silver had other ideas.

Trigger suddenly straightened up, dug his feet into the sand, starting running at breakneck speed, and launched off the edge of a dry arroyo. We gained altitude quicker than Skye ever thought about. If his run hadn't caused me to grab his front spine with a death grip, I would have tumbled off within moments of the launch.

After pulling his spine nearly off his back, I frantically pressed left and right to counteract his launch nearly straight up into the sky.

"Hey, slow down, Trigger! What's the matter with you? I'm new at this. Just slow down."

He rotated half way around to the left and I struggled to press hard to the right with my knee as I hung upside down. The dragon camp below was so far down, it looked like stick toys.

"Slam! What in the name of the demons are you doing? You aren't supposed to kill me first thing! Get your dad-blamed rear end turned back over so I won't fall off, you silver son of a..."

I squeezed my eyes shut and I only heard the roar of wind. I felt weightless. I must have lost my grip and I was falling. Unable to force my eyes open, I clenched my teeth waiting to splat on the ground.

Nothing. I couldn't tell up from down, but somehow it seemed I was seated on the back of Trigger again as my weight pressed down on my butt. I couldn't release the hold on his spine, but I finally forced my eyes open to a tiny squint. I saw blue, clouds, and the back of the silver dragon's head.

The cool wind dried my sweaty face and neck. Trigger tilted to the left and swooped downward on a gentle spiral. I just about peed my pants until we touched down as easy as a goose feather flying off a gander's back. That was close.

First, nearly crapping my pants riding on Skye. Now, almost wetting my pants on the back of this maniac Trigger!

Caerulus approached stomping the ground as if slamming puny humans into the sand like cockroaches. *That was the most ridiculous display of reckless stupidity I've ever seen done by dragon or man!*

Trigger stepped toward Caerulus so that he was between me and the big blue coming my way. At that point, I realized there was something very familiar about Trigger, but I couldn't think how. Was he among those who harassed Skye and me when we were hiding in her family cave a couple of years ago? No, that wasn't it. Could I remember a specific silver dragon that long ago? No. Caerulus stared at me bringing my attention back to the present.

"Yeah, I agree," I said, my voice cracking in a most unmanly way in spite of wanting to sound tough like my Dad. "But I was trying to get him under control like you trained me. It was the silver who ignored me and did all that crazy stuff way up there."

Don't blame the silver for your own recklessness and boyish foolhardiness darting all over the sky, Caerulus roared as Skye scrambled up next to him, her eyes reflecting as much sympathy for me as her mate showed anger at my incompetence.

Trigger turned his head far enough around to face me so that Caerulus and Skye couldn't see his face as he winked at me and smirked. I almost recalled where I saw him before, but it faded quickly.

"Me! I said it was..." Trigger's wink got through to me. He was messing with me like a schoolyard bully. He got me on his back and then took off like a brain-damaged humming bird as if it were me that was leading him around.

"Never mind," I said weakly. I looked to Skye for support. Her copper-flecked eyes looked down in disappointment. "Slam it all to blue blazes. Just forget it."

I turned to get out of sight of that smart aleck silver and Caerulus' white-hot anger. And Skye wasn't any help. Meanwhile, trigger flew off and disappeared in a matter of moments.

As I stumbled away, trying to keep from falling on my face, I sensed a flood of angry and frustrated thoughts from the blue dragons wash over me. I could recognize the pattern of Caerulus' stern emotions and Skye's outraged responses, but I had no clue what they were saying.

Dragon language. It wasn't even words, though I guess it carried meaning because the things that filled my head were patterns like waves crashing across the surface of Snow Lake in a storm.

Every once in a while, out of the storm of thoughts and emotions came something like my name. They were arguing about me. I'm sure by Skye's tone, she was standing up for me. And it was obvious how her mate felt.

When he expressed something along with my name it was with the same disdain and anger I heard in my father's voice when he was on a tirade about my stupidity and laziness. Or whatever set him off about me.

I tripped on the dead branch of an acacia tree but caught myself before I fell. I looked back to be sure the dragons didn't see my clumsiness. Glad no one saw me, I continued to walk away from the dragon's sight and wandered aimlessly, but not so far away I would get lost. I had a lot to think about. How I got here in this land of escaped dragons and all that I learned about this place filled my head as I wandered.

Later, I heard a whiz of wings overhead while a shadow of a dragon crossed the ground underneath my feet. I looked up to see another silver streaking in the direction of the feuding blues.

Curious, I turned back. Slowly, I became aware of Skye and Caerulus' agitation humming in my head much like katydids perched in our neighbors' trees back in Hilltop. I then heard a higher pitched voice interrupt the argument. More dragon language, no clue what the silver was saying but then I heard three familiar words, or rather, names: Baldric, Deryn, and Jarmil.

The blue dragon couple's children. What was this about? Nothing came into my mind as the dragon voices became quiet for several painful moments. I sensed Skye's emotions, steeped in concern and questioning.

I approached a small hill and could only see Caerulus and Skye's heads now. The young silver was out of sight below the edge of the hill. The two heads leaned into each other. The gentle motion of the two dragons sent a stab of fear in my heart about their children. Why? It was that tender gesture followed a few moments after what I thought was the high emotion of their argument about me.

I really liked those lively little dragons from the moment I helped them all escape enslavement back in Portville. Actually, they were not very little anymore. Baldric was nearly the size of a tall horse now, while Deryn, his younger sister, was about two thirds his size. Even little Jarmil was now as big as a half-grown pony.

Thoughts of them brought a smile to my face which kind of hurt because my skin was so dry from the desert air. I hadn't been in much of a smiling mood until right then. I turned my attention back to the blue dragon pair.

Their heads straightened and separated. I heard a more hopeful tone as the two blues raised their great wings, flapped thrice, and rose up over the desert heading in the direction of New Homestead Doom, where all the dragons new to Septrion lived.

I watched their forms as they shrank in size and darkened to nearly black as they flew away. A silver form rose up and followed them to the northwest.

Good. This whole sack full of manure concerning Trigger's stunt and Caerulus' fit about my stupidity just made me want to head south and keep going until I got back to Hilltop. But, instead, my curiosity and concern about Skye and Caerulus' children drew me back to their family cave. Was I ready to return deeper into the desert to the very edge of these empty lands, called Septrion by the dragons?

I don't know. On the other hand, I know I sure didn't want to head back to dear old Dad and his raging anger about one thing or another! Great Creator, was there anywhere I could go without all these arrows aiming for my butt?

At least Septrion was under the rebel dragons' wings and watchful eyes.

A couple of years ago, after I returned to Dad when Skye dropped me off at our farm, I was ready to give the farming life another chance. At least for a while.

As I walked, it all came back to me. Memories played out with exhausting drama like the ones presented by traveling actors during harvest festival time in Hilltop.

Slam!

TWO

Same Song, Different Verse

I really don't like drama. Don't get me wrong, I liked the plays the traveling actors troupe performed when they came through Hilltop. It's a great change from the same old boring chores and listening to my dad complain about everything, especially me.

At first, after Skye dropped me off, things were pretty good with Dad. I mean, we actually sat around the table in the morning and talked about stuff while we had a bit of bread and a hot cup of strong, black tea. I always liked mine with a drop of honey, but my father thought that was a stupid waste of the precious sweetener.

When I sneaked a spoonful into my cup, as usual, that first morning back, he saw me do it. He gave me that hard look of his like he does right before he blows up.

But he didn't. After his face tensed up, he relaxed, cracked a little smile, and motioned for me to sit down at the table.

"I guess I missed catching you steal a little something sweet for your tea these last couple of years," he said with a calm expression and soft tone of voice that didn't even sound like him. "I guess I thought there was only so much honey in the larder and we should save it. But for what? I don't bake the kind of things your mother did. Cakes, fancy breads, and even pastry when it was a special occasion."

"You and I don't have special occasions," I said with a bit of bitterness. "That's why I added a little something to make an otherwise miserable, cold morning a little better." I paused a little, wondering if I should say the next thing that popped into my mind.

My father watched the steam rise from his cup of tea and looked a touch sad. Wow, two expressions I never saw before on his face within a few moments of each other! So, why not say what popped into my head? Give it a shot.

"You never talked about my mother baking sweet things. That's kind of nice. I would have liked that. I wished she hadn't died." Oh great, now I've said too much. He always flew off the handle when I reminded him of her death.

But, nothing.

Well, almost nothing from him. This time his eyes seemed to get shiny. I got scared. Was he going to cry? I couldn't imagine him ever crying. Not ever, I'll bet that even when he was a baby, he probably set his chin in that stubborn way that I know all too well. Or he might have gritted his little toothless gums and sulked or made angry baby noises.

Thank goodness he didn't cry right in front of me. Instead, he smiled a little more and started talking in a voice so soft that, for a moment, I thought someone else in the kitchen was talking.

"Your mother was a wonderful cook. Baking was her specialty. Everyone in Hilltop headed straight for her cakes and things when we had a social in the church.

"You went to church?" I blurted out.

"Yeah, I know. Hard to believe. Things were different when she was alive. When I was home..." He stopped cold and looked at me with suspicion. Then he went a little vague like he forgot what he was going to say. "Anyway. Let's get this tea in our bellies. We have work to do. We'll get breakfast later after the cows are milked."

His face went back to its usual scowl and he slurped the steaming tea down like he was drinking hot nails. I shut up and wondered if I had imagined the whole thing.

Yet, it was okay. He didn't yell at me the rest of that day and for many days, even weeks after that. Until I screwed up. I had to know something, so one night, while we ate supper with our usual lack of talking, I broke the silence like a dad-blamed fool.

"Dad, I'd like to know something."

"What?" he said almost irritated that I disturbed a perfectly wonderful stillness.

"I don't understand how the town folk said nothing after I disappeared for all those days when I took off with Skye, uh, you know, the dragon."

He looked at me like I was some bandit that had suddenly appeared in our kitchen. "Skye? The dragon? What else did you do? Your usual soft-headed business of giving that dragon a name like it was some pet?"

"No. She..." Did I really want to tell him everything about the dragons? That they talk, at least in their heads, and some weird guy like me could hear their thoughts? And all that stuff about their families?

My dad's look changed from considering me as an intruder to his annoying punk of a son. "So, what is it you want to tell me?"

"Not really anything. I want to know what the people around here wondered about me when I just up and disappeared. I mean everybody must have known about the dragon disappearing instead of just dying out there on the tracks."

He looked back at his cup of tea and half-eaten plate of food, seeming to gather himself to explain something to me that I should have known in the first place.

"Oh yeah, the whole town knew something was up. They all came over here asking about you. That crew of deputies from the train company asked everyone what happened to the kid and the blue dragon. They went into

Emerald Forest figuring the dragon was trying to get back to its caves. Most everyone around here knows the dragons used to live in a bunch of caves a few miles from here.

"That was back before the Dragon Wars got bad," he continued. He blew on his tea and took a sip. "At first, some of the people that went down to see the dragon dying were saying the dragon must have faked exhaustion to fool you into helping it get away. Others said you were threatened with death and were probably dead, a small meal in the belly of that beast.

"But I got the truth from old Mr. Henry. I was mighty mad you had up and left. Especially after I told you to get back to work when I saw you down there at the station. Just running off from your chores like that!" His voice reached its usually loud rant. But in the blink of an eye, his angry face dropped. He took another sip.

"Anyway, old Henry said he saw you with that dragon headed for the forest. Said you claimed the dragon was just our workhorse. He believed you for a while until he saw the dragon's giant footprints leading down the forest trail. Then he heard about the commotion at the station with the dragon collapsing and disappearing afterwards."

"Oh, demons of Hades," I said without stopping myself from blurting it out. "So that was it. Old Henry could see that I was fine and that I told him a big fib about the horse following me into the forest."

"Of course," my father growled. "He may be old but he's not stupid. In fact, you should be gall-darned grateful that I had the presence of mind to tell him to keep his mouth shut. I was the only one he told about your little stunt."

"Really? That's a relief, but didn't everyone else kind of figure things out? At least that I disappeared because of the dragon? Were there any other stories about me?"

"Yeah, there were stories! Are you some kind of fool? It's all people could talk about for weeks on end. Some thought you were dead. Others had the idea you got protective toward dragons like you do every other beast in the whole valley."

"What did *you* say about me?" At that point, I didn't even care that I was egging him on to get madder and madder.

"I just thought—" He stopped and stared at the wall across the table. For a moment I thought he saw something crawling up the wall. I glanced that way. Only our shadows moved across the stains and dents from a long hard life in a cramped little farmhouse.

Dad took a breath and continued. "I just thought you had gone soft in the head and wanted to rescue another useless animal. But then, I thought about it and knew better. I, too, have been among the dragons."

"So, you *did* go off to the army when you were young right near the end of the Dragon Wars. I didn't realize that, but in a way, it makes sense. Other people in Hilltop talk about the war even though you never told me anything. I mean, most young guys joined the army in those days. So, I can understand how you might hate the dragons, and all."

"I don't *hate* the dragons. But I don't trust them either. You don't have any clue what it's like to go to war. It's horrible. All the death and destruction. There were some friends of mine that... well, they got burned by dragon fire or torn apart by dragon claws. Some died. It's not something I want to talk about."

I avoided looking him in the eye. "Sorry, I didn't really mean to bring that up. I just wanted to know why no one let the train people know that I was involved somehow with Skye—uh, well, the dragon."

"Sure, you do. I would. I don't blame the dragons for all of the war and all the horrible things," Dad said raising his voice. "We—humans—did some bad things, too. I couldn't stand it. After a while, I came home. I did my part."

"All right. I sort of understand. I mean, that's something I don't really know about, you know, how horrible it must have been." I wanted to shut up, but I couldn't stop myself.

I went on, "I guess if I had been alive then, I would have done the same thing. But I got to know the dragons in a much different way just because I was curious about the dragon dying down there on the tracks. And then she wasn't so bad and I—just like you said—got soft and wanted to help."

My father actually chuckled. If I hadn't held a steaming cup of tea, I would have fallen to the floor in shock.

Then he said, "I don't think the dragons were doing a bad thing by fighting us. I saw they were suffering, too, in the war. At least what I saw. I wasn't so set against animals like you might think, so I saw them as big old snakes or lizards but also a lot like cows and horses. A hell of a lot bigger, meaner, and more dangerous than farm animals, but they had families and friends, and I could see they suffered too."

He shook his head and continued. "I just wanted to get away from all the death and destruction. I was wounded, so it was a good time to come home. I already knew your mother before I went off, and I thought someday we would be together. But not if I died or got burned on the battlefield fighting dragons."

He stopped, finished his tea and said, "That's it. That's all I'm going to say. The whole town believed you should be protected from the train people and so they shut up. I'm glad it's over and let's get to work. We're burning sunlight."

That conversation was the closest I had ever been with my dad. Too bad, but after speaking our hearts to each other, we kind of clammed up.

Very quickly, we fell back into our old ways of dealing with each other except for a couple of things. He didn't quite treat me like a punk anymore. But he still got mad and complained about most everything I did, but it was strange how he did it.

He wouldn't tell me anything to my face. Like when I forgot to move another pile of hay down to the barn floor to spread around the cow and horse stalls so they wouldn't have to stomp around in their own manure so much.

He just came into the barn while I was acting like I was busy. He looked around and said, "Huh!" like somebody had kicked him in the stomach. Then he would leave the barn and I could hear him mutter under his breath about "Good for nothing, lazy bum. Why do I have to do everything and remind him of everything!"

I got the message and scurried up the ladder to the loft and pitched a big pile of hay down to the floor and busted my butt shoveling out the old soiled manure and hay so I could replace it with the fresh hay.

The other thing was talking about dragons. After I had been back home a few months, I started talking about how bad the train company treated the dragons.

"Here we go again with your bleeding-heart whining about how the dragons are abused!" he announced to the chickens and goats.

"Dad, please!"

"Oh, don't 'Dad please' me! The dragons got a right to be on their own, but that doesn't mean you have to stick your nose in their business. Especially when they want to escape and then come back to stir up more trouble. Those wars were horrible, I tell you. It was horrible for both sides and I sure don't want anyone to know I've got a traitor for a son!"

"I am not a traitor! Wanting to help the dragons be free isn't going to turn me against people! At least... not all people."

"So, you say, Mr. Smarty Mouth. But just what do you expect? For everyone, especially the train company and their deputies to roll over and say, 'Oh, my Heavens! Let's free the dragons and forget about having trains move people and things around this little country of ours! Let's just love the dragons that have burned our homes, people, and lives!'"

"You're making this a bigger thing than it is. Oh, never mind! I've finished my slave-labor for today, so I'm going to town. I may not be back—at all or for a good while!"

"Good," he crowed as I stomped off down through our field towards town.

We both got pretty hot that time. I just wanted quiet because there was no point in going on and on about something I thought we would never agree on.

Besides, it was a good excuse to go talk to the postman about the day Skye collapsed on the tracks and why the train deputies didn't find out who I was.

When I knocked on the train station door, it creaked open from the force of my knock. "Hello, anyone here?"

"Who else would be here?" the old postman said as he turned around from his desk, piled high with mail, packages, and a thick film of dust over the lower layers of clutter. "Oh, it's you, Jaiden. How's things on the farm now that you're back?"

"Well, not so great, Mr. Alden. My Dad..."

He chuckled and smoothed his thick moustache. "If you two were singing church songs together, that would be a gal-durned shocker. But getting along? Hah!"

"Yeah? Well, you're right about that. We're like a duet singing this song—no, better yet, we're *dueling* this same song, but now we've got a new verse to fuss over."

I shook my head and kicked a pebble out the door, "I kind of wished I was ready to start building a little hut and working my own land, but... it's different now that I'm back. Things aren't the same." I lingered for several moments, not knowing how to ask my burning question.

He smiled and turned back to a stack of papers on his desk. "What's on your mind, son?"

I hesitated. Then decided to go for it.

"I want to know why people in the town aren't asking me about being gone. Even in church, people are friendly but they just say 'hello' and then walk away without asking anything."

I mentioned church because Mr. Alden was also the local minister on Saturdays and Sundays, so he witnessed what I was talking about.

He got up slowly, allowing his old body time to stretch mostly upright. "We aren't fools, Jaiden. We know you went off with the dragon. I'm sure your dad said something about it to you, but it's true. No one here is in love with the train company. Especially those hoodlums they call deputies that go around keeping the train dragons in line, carting off their bodies when they die of exhaustion, and harassing plain folks if they complain about how they use the dragons."

"I had no idea," I said, trying to get my breath. "I thought I was the only one who felt sorry for the dragons."

"It's not that we feel sorry for dragons and want them to come and cuddle up with us. It's just—well, it's a matter of freedom. Certainly, none of us have the nerve to resist the train deputies. They know how to use those weapons of theirs and those big booming metal tubes they call cannons."

He took a couple of steps right up to me. "We don't want any more war with the dragons. And, yes, we're afraid to go against the train company because the government in Portville has the soldiers and the power to make our lives miserable if we fight back or complain about dragon abuse. I'm sorry, that's probably not what you want to hear."

"No, I understand. It's scary—I mean I don't know about war. But while I was with the dragons, I saw a fight between some of those dragons used by the train company and... uh, the dragons I was with who were trying to escape the Big Barn. It's not something I would want to get in the middle of."

I sighed and felt a little light-headed. "I guess I'm not any different from the rest of you. But I don't want to see bad things happen to any creatures or people. You know?"

"Yeah, I know, son," Mr. Alden said. "It's OK. We all kept our mouths shut and just acted like the stupid country folk those deputies think we are and didn't say anything about you when they came around asking."

"I guess that's all I wanted to know. Thanks."

THREE

Dragon Lover

On the way home, I felt light. My feet barely touched the ground I was in such a good mood. That doesn't happen often, so I immersed myself in the warm feeling that started in my chest and spread throughout my body as I practically flew up the hills back to our farm.

Of course, my father would quickly throw a cold bucket of water on that, but it was good while it lasted. As I swung a leg over the rock wall to our pasture, I heard a shuffling behind me. I turned to see a small figure in a dark, hooded cloak that reached the muddy ground.

"What—" I started to say.

"Oh, sorry, I didn't mean to scare you," a girl's quiet voice said.

"You didn't scare me, I just thought I was alone. How long have you been following me?"

The cloak shifted around as small fingers reached up to the hood and pulled it down to reveal the face of Alden's daughter. At that moment, I couldn't remember her name. She was about three or four years younger than me, so it wasn't like she was a part of my small group of old school friends.

"Oh, it's you," I said, still searching for a name. I thought it was something like her father's name, but not quite. "I guess you saw me talking to your father at the train station."

"Kind of. I was bringing him lunch Mama fixed for him. I saw you leave. I... sorry, I shouldn't have followed you like that. I just wanted..."

"What? I'm not going to bite you, silly girl."

She looked a bit insulted at me calling her "silly girl," but so what? That's what she was.

"If you forgot, my name is Aleena."

"Oh, yeah, I knew that." Of course, I hadn't remembered, but how could I keep track of every kid's name in Hilltop? "So, anyway..." How do I get rid of her without being really rude?

Without missing a beat, she went on. "I haven't seen you since you, uh, came back. You know, from the dragons."

I sighed. "I suppose everybody knows I went off with a dragon. But you don't know the whole story and I'm not going to tell it to you."

She looked even more disappointed at that remark.

"I mean," I continued, "I'm not going to tell anyone about it. It's not something a lot of people should know because it'll just get spread around and the wrong ears might hear something they shouldn't."

"Oh, no! They won't hear anything about it from me. I promise. I know how dangerous that could be. I'm just, uh, curious. You know?" she said meekly.

"Well, there's not much to talk about," I lied. I really wanted to move on. She was starting to annoy me standing there looking at me like I was some god dropped out of the sky. I mean, I could be wrong, but she sure was giving me the eye in a way I never noticed before.

Of course, I never noticed much about her before, anyway. Just another pesky little girl I saw around school and the rare times I had been in church lately.

"Look," I said starting to turn away from her. "I gotta go. My dad will kick my butt if I don't get the rest of my chores done. All right, uh, Aleena?"

"Oh, sure. Sorry, didn't want to bother you. Maybe some other time." She paused as if hoping I would stay a little longer and tell her something fantastic about dragons.

I didn't. "Yeah, some other time. Bye."

"Bye," she said, the disappointment frosting her voice and face like an ice-cold morning.

I avoided running into my father as I approached the barn carefully and entered. Not there. Good. I then went about my business until dark.

I gobbled down the meager bean soup we had for supper. Its blandness was only saved by a yeasty slab of bread. I smeared one last dab of butter on the crust and savored it's salty toastiness. Now that my stomach was full, I could risk being run off from the table and not starve overnight.

"So, Father," I seldom called him, Father, guaranteeing he would look up and actually make eye contact with me. "Tell me about your time with the dragons. How that all happened?"

His gaze went from wide-open eyes that gradually narrowed to mere slits. Tilting his head back, he muttered, "Why do you want to know? How is that your business?"

I figured since I had him stirred up, might as well go whole hog as he would say. "It's my business because I was with the dragons and you said the other day how you had something to do with them and how you didn't think they deserved the way they've been treated."

I thought his look would pierce my eyes, right through my brain and out the back of my head. But it didn't. He quickly directed his attention to his nearly empty bowl of beans.

"I don't really want to—" he mumbled.

Here it comes.

"What I mean is. I don't want you talking about this to every little worthless hoodlum around here."

"I promise. It's no one else's business especially since everyone already knows about my time with the dragons. I have no one I want to talk to about it except you."

"Then this is it. And there'll be no more talk of it." He looked back up at me and, once again, his eyes bore right through my head. I nodded meekly.

He cleared his throat, ate the last spoonful of beans and took a deep draught of warm tea. His gaze lifted up to where the bare wall facing him met the dark timbers of the ceiling. He began to talk in a low voice.

It all started when I got the bright idea of using silver dragons around the farm when your mother's old horse died. I needed something to pull the wagon and maybe a plow, too. It wasn't long after the Dragon Wars were over and the army started using some of the captive dragons for heavy work on farms and construction. The blues were too big for this little plot of land but a silver or two could come in handy.

So, I up and went down the hill toward Portville. Of course, I didn't expect to go that far. I figured some of the other towns on down close to the Nulland Plains would have some captive dragons available for sale. I first heard about such a thing from Alden the postman. He knew more about the news of the world than anyone around.

Well, when I got there—I believe the name of the village was Dry Creek—I found a livery stable that had a couple of silvers tied up outside.

"Son, you come to the right place," the army guy said to me. He was in charge of handling and training the dragons to work. "Let me show you what a silver can do."

He went over the corral fence and grabbed a long rope that was tied around one of the dragon's necks. There was also a wide band of leather wrapped all around the dragon's body to hold his wings tight so he couldn't fly.

I tell you that silver was hopping mad. He reared up his head, opened his wide mouth, and hissed louder than a copperhead snake that's been kicked in the face. It scared the Hades out of me! But his feet were hobbled so he couldn't take more than a short step. That trainer unhitched a long whip out of his belt and snapped it in the dragon's face.

More hissing and shuffling around the little corral, I tell you that silver scared me bad, but the handler paid it no mind. He snapped the whip again. That time he laid it on the dragon's back and up the side of his head.

The poor creature slung his head around trying to get away from that whip. And then he made a sound... I can't forget that sound. It was like a child crying out of pain and fear. But the handler just walked up to the dragon and placed his boot against his ribs and knocked the silver to the ground. And that silver wasn't much smaller than a horse.

There it was squirming all over the place, stirring up the hay and manure trying to get away from that mean, son of a—

I tell you, it was funny, but not laughing funny. I just felt sick. Like I was going to pass out. Me, a grown man, ready to keel over like a scared girl! And not only that, but I was afraid the dragon would heave itself around that tight little corral and knock the fence right into me.

But the handler took up the slack of the rope and brought the dragon right up to his face and yelled, "Come on, you silver devil. You want to try to take me out? Go ahead and see what it'll get you!"

He struck the dragon right in the face with the handle of his whip. The dragon lay down and stayed there in the filthy dirt and breathed heavily and—I don't know if it was possible but it... whimpered. I couldn't believe my ears.

As mad as that dragon was before—now it whimpered.

All I could think about was how I volunteered to fight the dragons even though I was very young at the time. And now I was ready to fight for them, but it was too late. That war was over and done.

You know better than anyone I don't put much stock in treating animals like pets. But I just couldn't stand the way that guy, that beast, treated the silver dragon. And I did it. I opened my big mouth.

"What in all the Hells of the Underground are you doing?" I yelled. "That animal doesn't deserve this kind of treatment. I'm a farmer and no pussyfoot when it comes to getting animals to work, but cruelty won't get you anywhere. You're no farmer because you're taking this too far. You don't hurt the animals you depend on to survive. Besides, dragons aren't meant for this kind of thing."

"Oh, yeah, mister! You're just a dumb-butt hayseed that knows nothing about handling these dragons. Someday, we're going to have them doing all kinds of things. Maybe even towing people around in wagons or something. But you'll just be stuck on your farm coddling your little farm animals while we go out and take over the world!"

"Well, that's fine for you, but I don't want to have anything to do with it and I can guarantee no other farmers are going to come around looking to put dragons to work."

"Good! We don't need your kind sticking your nose in a man's business. And you can tell anyone else in your little hole-in-the-ground town that dragons are none of your business. If you or your type come around here again, you'll all find yourselves with halters strapped on, working side-by-side with the dragons. Get!"

And I walked right out of there and hiked a good ten miles the rest of that day just to get away. By the time folks around Hilltop heard about it, a lot of them shunned me. They called me, of all people, a Dragon Lover!

But the few who weren't interested in having anything to do with dragons or those government and company types in Portville or Dry Creek or wherever... well, they just kept quiet about it!

Everybody knew there'd been some dragons living up in the high hills east of town for the longest time, but they never bothered us, and we didn't have anything to do with them. Eventually, when the big shots in Portville started up the dragon trains, folks were more put-out about Hilltop being left behind when it came to traveling on the trains. No one really cared about how the dragons were being used.

For years most everyone kept away from me. So, piss on them! I just wanted to be left alone. That's the way it was for quite a while until more people around here realized the government and the train company were nothing but trouble, so we had as little to do with them as possible.

That's when most everyone came around to my way of thinking.

This was all before you were born. In fact, even before your mother and I got interested in each other. She—well, she thought that...

Huh! I don't know what she was thinking. And now here I have a son who loves dragons! I'm not going to talk about it anymore. Get your chores done and get to bed and forget all about this crap, gal-dang it!

The evening ended rather abruptly when my father got up and knocked the table away from him spilling both our cups of tea. He glared at me for what seemed an eternity. Then he pointed his finger in my face like it was a crossbow, loaded and ready to release. His mouth opened and closed like a dying fish pulled out of a stream. I could tell he still had something to say, but all I heard was a gurgling sound in his throat.

He turned on his heel and stormed out. All sorts of banging and clattering emerged from his bedroom. But I acted as if he didn't exist as I cleaned up the mess, rinsed off the dishes and withdrew outside to put the animals into the barn and complete the day's chores.

Later, I slunk into the house and retreated to my bed and lamp table around the corner from the fireplace. I had a lot to think about.

Time passed and the two of us found ourselves in a situation where we lived like two prisoners who had to share a small space while they despised each other. So, we avoided any discussion that would lead to a fight.

Days became weeks and weeks turned into months. Nearly two years of the same old thing went by before I finally faced the fact that I had a decision to make.

FOUR

Motherly Treatment

I couldn't savor the pleasant air of Fall while I milked our cow. Somehow the rhythm of squeezing the milk out of the old heifer didn't give me that same sense of calm and a job well-done. In fact, nothing satisfied me.

Just as I was about to pass out from nearly two years of boredom and self-loathing, I heard a voice. So soft, I didn't understand the words at first.

Something sounded familiar about that voice.

"Who's there?" I called out thinking it surely couldn't be my father.

Then a strong, feminine voice answered. *Are you ready to have a little excitement come into your life, Jaiden?* I knew immediately that it was Skye.

Skye!

Yes, of course. It's me and I'm wondering if you've finally had enough of this farmer's life and are ready for adventure?

"By the Creator of all that's in the world and Heaven, Yes! Take me away."

Not so fast. You need to finish milking the cow and then say goodbye to your father. We aren't going to do this like we did the first time.

"I wouldn't worry about being polite with him. He's—"

No discussion. Finish your work. Take me to your father so I can assure him all will be well if you go with me.

"Anything would be better than these endless chores and life with him!"

She didn't answer. I looked around. She wasn't in the barn because she probably couldn't fit in our small building.

"OK." I looked toward the open barn door. "Let's play by your rules. I'm almost done and then I want to see you. Then I'll tell my dear old Dad I'm leaving."

Don't rush. Do a good job and don't neglect anything before you take your leave.

"I guess this is what it's like to have a mother," I fumed. Then I chuckled at the thought and my childish attitude.

As soon as I made sure all the animals were tucked away in their stalls, watered, with fresh oats to snack on, and the barn doors shut and latched, I headed for the house. I poured the milk in a big pottery jar, sealed the lid and took it to our cellar below the kitchen to chill.

Back up in the kitchen, I heard Dad rummaging around in his room before he came out and grunted at me. That was his charming way of asking me to warm up left-over cornbread and ham stew. I thought twice about making my announcement before supper since ham stew was one of the rare and really good meals I enjoyed.

After supper and our bowls and cups were put away, I turned to say my piece. He was already heading for his bed.

"Father—Dad, I have something to say to you."

He turned slowly and stared at me. His brow wrinkled as he grunted. Facing him, I knew I had to address him as an adult, an equal. Not a kid.

"What?" he said roughly.

"I'm going back to the dragons. Skye is here. I don't know what's going on, but I told her I didn't want to be left out if they were going to start something big to gain their true freedom. Not just go off running to some hole in the ground to hide from people. Well, I didn't exactly say all that, but she and I understood each other."

"What in Hades did you not learn from nearly getting yourself killed or thrown in jail for gallivanting off with those beasts and how in the blue blazes can you talk to a dragon?"

"Never mind how I talk to her. We have a way of, I don't know, *understanding* each other. And another thing,

I didn't have your experience in war. But I thought you understood a little bit from that experience with the cruel handler in Dry Creek. I can't let it go. I can't pretend what happens out there to the dragons is none of my business."

His face suddenly dropped from white hot anger to maybe a kind of sadness. Sad because he thought he was going to lose me.

I continued before I lost my courage. "Why would you think I want to stay? This isn't the life I want to lead until I end up as bitter and lonely as you."

Now, that's enough. Skye's voice cut right into my thoughts as if she were next to me in our tight little kitchen. I tried not to answer because it was enough my father thought I was stupid. I didn't want him thinking I was crazy, too.

"Sorry," I nearly whispered. "That wasn't what I meant to say—"

"But you thought it," Dad said. He sat down heavily and rested his hands on the table. He turned them over and inspected the rough calluses and cuts from the hard work of farming.

I tried to fill the big silence that suffocated me. "I can't explain everything. I wanted to a couple of years ago, but you cut off all discussion of dragons. I want to say they're not just beasts. They are smart. Smarter than we are in a lot of ways, but they don't make things like people do. Tools and houses and such. But they think and they feel."

Dad looked at me, I could tell he was convinced I was crazy just by his expression.

"So, I'm going," I said. "I'll stay the night. But—"

"No. Not until I explain something about your mother. What I was going to say when you came back year before last. But I couldn't—"

I was so stunned, I blurted out, "All the years and times I've begged and prayed you would tell me more about her. And about you, too. How both of you were, and all. What she thought of me and how she took care me when I was a baby! And *now* you want to have a heart-to-heart with me!"

"Fine. Have it your way. I'll say no more."

"Isn't that just the way you've always been about her with me." I gathered my wild thoughts trying to think straight. Do I miss this chance to find out more about Mother? I've got to try. "All right. I'll sit and listen," I said, my voice shaking.

"Oh, no you don't. Too late. Go, now. Don't wait for morning."

"Thank the Creator! Then I'm gone!"

I stalked out into the dark, cold night. I heard a rustling of a giant's wings and the rough shuffling of big, clawed feet.

You're not going with me or any dragon if you can't leave in a civil manner.

"Geeze, you are being my mom! I always felt deprived of motherly treatment when I watched my friends around their mothers. Now, I'm not particularly interested in the experience anymore."

You go back in there and leave on a better footing or I'm flying.

"OK. OK. I'll try."

I did. But it didn't do any good. Dad just sat there and continued to stare at his hands as if they belonged to someone else.

"Whether the dragons want me or not. I'm going. Bye."

"I've already said my good-byes. Go," he said in an eerily quiet voice that scared me more than his most angry rants.

I grabbed what little possessions I thought I wanted, wrapped them up in a thick old blanket and turned my back on my bed to leave. I remembered my slingshot and reached under the bed, gathered it and my rock bag, stuffed it in my blanket roll, and stalked out. I was tempted to slam the door, but resisted since Skye was outside waiting.

At least I thought she was.

The night felt as empty as my heart.

Gone.

Ah well, I needed a good run to burn off the anger, frustration, and loss. I ran aimlessly. I fell twice stumbling on rocks like some child having a temper tantrum. Finally, I climbed the hill north of the farm, pulling myself up the rough slope until the cuts and bruises on my hands and legs forced the bad feelings out of my body.

At the top, I slowed and walked, unsteady and unsure of where I was going.

Finally, in the dark of night, the flapping of wings the size of sails filled the sky above my head before Skye landed in front of me.

FIVE

Long Flight to Another World

I loved flying again. More than two years ago, before I met Skye, I would have laughed my butt off if someone told me I would love to fly. Crazy! But there I was, soaring through the moonlit night grinning like a drunken donkey. That is, if donkeys drank ale.

The moonlight was just bright enough that I could tell when the dark forest was no longer below. We flew over a barren plain filled with strange looking hills with a flat top. Never saw those around Hilltop, in the Emerald Forest or even across the Nulland Plains.

My heart jumped into my throat as we headed for a landing at the foot of one of the big hills with a flat top. Skye set down on the dark side into a black nothingness but she must have landed on something solid.

The dragon pulled in her wings. She didn't move and the wind no longer blew in my face but I wasn't about to let go of the strap around her middle. I was surrounded by darkness, except moonglow slipping over the flat top of the massive hill on our left.

Well? Are you getting off or do you want to fly some more?

"No. How long did this take, nearly all night? I loved flying but I got tired of the cold wind."

Good news. We're done. You need to dismount and help take off my strap. When we first arrived here, Caerulus figured out how to remove my strap using the claws at the joint on the leading edge of his wings. I haven't had it on since then almost two years ago. He said it was much harder to put on than to take off. And I feel freer with that reminder of my captivity off my back.

"That's good to hear. I'll take it off for you but, first, where do I step? I can't see the ground or much of anything!"

The ground is where it's always been. As she turned her head toward me. I saw a little smirk cross her lips. *I'll lay down on my stomach so it'll be a short step.* She paused a few moments but I didn't move. *Come on, do it. What do you think I'm standing on?*

"Okay, okay. I'll get off but I better not fall on my face."

If you do, you're going to need more training than I thought.

"Training? What are you talking about?"

Another voice, lower in pitch and impatient, spoke in my head. *If you're joining us in our cause, you will have to make yourself useful. It would be nice to have a farmer to grow better food, but we need human hands and faces for more important work. You're the first one to join us, so—*

"Caerulus! I recognized that voice in my head. How are you? Honestly, I didn't think about you when Skye picked me up. I just thought about getting out of Hilltop and away from my Dad—again!"

I'm fine, but we don't have much time for happy reunions. If you're sincere about helping our cause and you 'don't want to miss out,' as you told Skye when we dropped you off back at your farm, then it's time to get on with it.

Well, there's nothing like cutting through the social crap. He was right, I had said that. And I had jumped on Skye's back to bring me to the dragons' desert lands. Time to put up or shut up as Dad would say.

So, are you getting off my mate's back or not? Caerulus insisted.

I loosened my grip on Skye's leather strap and gently reached my left foot down. I touched solid ground almost immediately. Once on both feet, I slowly let go of the strap.

"Which way do I go from here?" I said in a shaky voice.

If you could take off my strap first, I would appreciate it.

That was easy enough. "Done."

Then follow us, Skye said soothingly. *Our home cave is only a few minutes' walk from here. And don't worry, we'll be out in the light of the moon so you can see the ground as we walk. Only the first few steps are tricky.*

It was as she said. Yet, I began to feel exposed to danger walking across this open and flat land. Only scrappy little things passed for trees, barely taller than me and nothing like the full, tall trees in the Emerald Forest. These trees' skinny branches and twigs reached to the sky as if pleading for mercy.

Soon, Skye said, *Our home cave is ahead.*

As we approached, I saw their cave faced the moon so it was an easy entrance into its depths which were quite dark. I darted into the cave quickly, wishing to get out of sight.

Over here in the shaft of light, Skye said. *You don't have to hunker down in the darkness. There are no silvers or golds sneaking about in the service of our human enemies.*

What a relief. A pile of furry skins tucked in an oval depression in the floor made a nice little bed just my size. With a nod of her head, Skye motioned me to lie down. As soon as I stretched out on the soft furs, Skye and Caerulus excused themselves, leaving me alone as they went deeper into the cavern to check on their children.

I wanted to see the youngsters again, but I didn't realize how tired I was after clinging onto Skye's side for most of the flight. I fell asleep in moments and didn't stir until the warm sun peeked into the cave and greeted me with a brilliant yellow glare in my eyes.

It was strangely quiet. Did I dream that Skye flew me to this alien land?

SIX

Walkabout

A s I drifted into the main living area, I saw Skye sitting quietly. Her eyes barely open, gazed across the barren land beyond the cavern entrance.

Looking around I noticed right away that Caerulus wasn't around and I heard the high-pitched sounds of young dragons playing down the slope from the cave.

Skye's eyes opened wide, saw me, and smiled a toothy dragon smile.

Oh, here you are, she said. *I was awake but my mind was a thousand miles and years away. But never mind that. You must be hungry. Let me bring you something to eat.*

I brought out the fur pieces I slept on and sat cross-legged, ready to eat a cow's leg. As she set a pile of roots and some kind of dried mystery meat in front of me, I started to say something offhand about breakfast, but thought better of it. I recalled she didn't often understand human sarcasm.

In any case, it was good to see Skye again away from my grouchy father. The bad part was the lousy dragon food. It brought back memories of hiding out with Skye when she first took me to her old family cave.

Back then, we had only a few small animals and various wild vegetables and root stock to eat while we hid out in that cave. Funny, I had forgotten that part. At least I helped them figure out how to flash cook their meat with their renewed power of spitting flames. For all the unpleasantness living with my father, we ate pretty good on the farm. Plain food, but much better than the food in that cave.

After a bland and slightly bitter breakfast, Skye took me on a short tour to see the rest of the community they call Septrion. She and I agreed it would be easier to walk since she didn't want the strap around her middle after I removed it the night before. As we walked along the base of the hill, we came to an open space and all around us were dozens of these flat-topped hills.

I can see you're puzzled by this land of ours. These rocky hills are called mesas by the dragons who first settled here.

She then explained how dragons made this lonely desert of sand, rocks, and mesas their own town.

Years before we arrived here, the old warriors and escaped blue dragons found their way to this place and formed weyrs.

"What's that?" I asked.

Traditionally, all of us who were related, either directly or a few generations back, are called a weyr. The place in the forest near Hilltop where you and I stayed is my clan's weyr called D'laire Lodge. But in this land, dragons who escaped human captivity formed a weyr which we call New Homestead. Caerulus and I named our family cave, Azure Den.

A few miles away is the community called Founders Weyr. The dragons who always lived free—and fled after the end of the Dragon Wars—settled there.

"I had no idea," I said.

She stopped at the edge of a red sandstone mesa. *Here we are at the Brothers' Dwelling.* She motioned with her chin toward an oval-shaped opening in the side of the cliff.

She hissed loudly followed by words that flooded my head. *Luc and Owyn! Come forth. This is Skye of Azure Den.*

A voice answered, *It is I, Owyn. Please enter the cave of your friends.*

I followed along behind Skye in case they jumped to the conclusion that a human had fooled them to gain entry into their private domain. Sure enough, a dragon somewhat smaller than Skye rushed forward as he reared back his head.

Stop, Owyn! This is a friend. Jaiden is the human I told you about who helped me free my family. He is here to assist us in our cause for freedom.

The dragon stopped short, stretched out his neck toward me while lowering his head to my level.

Hmm. A fine-looking young man, that is for a human. I see you didn't draw back in fear of me. Commendable.

Coming around from behind him, a slightly bigger dragon spoke in a calm voice. *I can see he has a different aspect about him. As if he is among friends and not impressed by our size and appearance.* His lips parted showing his shiny long teeth. I think it was a smile. *I am Luc, older brother of Owyn. Welcome to our modest cave.*

I swallowed hard, hoping I could keep up the so-called fearless impression I made. I surely didn't want to answer in a shaky voice. "I have become accustomed to dragons due to the friendly manners of Skye, Caerulus, and their young ones. I hope to be of service."

Both dragons nodded their heads and stepped aside so I could enter their cave which didn't extend but a few feet beyond the entrance. It was wide and roomy though.

We had a pleasant visit while I learned they were both wagon dragons on a big farm much like the one where Skye's father, Dark Cloud, and his family spent their early days in captivity.

Luc explained, *Although Dark Cloud's attempt to lead his family to freedom failed, the story passed among blue dragons all over the farming lands and canyons for years.*

"How is that possible?" I asked.

To this day, Luc said, *humans don't know we can communicate with each other through our minds. The word spread among the dragons at the farm where Skye's family lived and then through the years over the fence of one farm to another as wagon dragons were moved about. Finally, the story came to us, and it gave us the idea to try ourselves.*

Owyn picked up the story. *We learned that Dark Cloud attempted to escape by secretly loosening the tree trunks that formed the walls of the dragon barns and to sneak out during a human winter celebration. We were lucky enough to use the same trick. Since we were able to release each other's wing harnesses, we flew away one night.*

Luc made a jolly gurgling sound and said, *Yes, it was funny. Of course, our clipped wings kept us from flying any higher than about ten feet. However, once we were past the fences and headed for the hills, no human was able to see us on the horizon as we wove our way through narrow canyons.*

Owyn gurgled even louder. *We flew and flew, guessing which way was north. After three days of wandering, we made it here.*

The two brothers twisted around on the floor gurgling and hissing. I guess that was their version of a laughing fit.

After they settled down and accepted congratulations from me, Skye said we had to move on.

We enjoyed your visit, Owyn said. *You're the first human we've felt good about. Please drop by again.*

We continued across an open area between mesas. I took in the expanse thinking this was a perfect place for dragons to settle down away from human interference.

Sure I thought it was too bleak and dead, but at least they were free.

"So how did you hear about this land?" I asked Skye.

Right at that moment, Caerulus flew overhead and came down to join our tour of the weyr.

I heard part of your conversation, he said. *The Founders sent a few silvers to sneak into places like Portville and the dragon training camps to tell us of their existence. The silvers only speak a few simple words but it was enough to give us hope even if we considered it more wishful thinking than reality. Many of us in the dragon train camps agreed that whoever could gain freedom, would head north.*

"And sure enough, here you all are. I like that."

Yes, it is good, Skye said, *but now we want more than simple freedom. We want to live in places like our old homes in the forested hills because desert living is hard.*

Even the tough old Founders agree with that, Skye's mate added. *Soon, our time will come. We have enough dragons from various slave camps: the train dragons, construction workers, those who help in war, farm workers, wagon dragons—*

Even though I had heard the words "wagon dragons" before, I couldn't help laughing out loud. Caerulus gave me a harsh look.

"Sorry, just stupid *human humor*—oh, now *I'm* rhyming words," I snickered.

Both dragons looked at me like I had fallen out of a hayloft.

"*Human humor*—get it? People amuse themselves making silly rhymes." I continued, "You, know, where words sound similar like in a poem or song."

We don't rhyme our songs, Skye said simply.

I throttled my giggling and forced a serious look.

We continued our tour of the area, giving me a chance to meet more recently escaped dragons including one pair of mates, Venturo and Marisol, and their daughter Carina.

We had barely stepped inside this family's cozy cave when the male dragon took up their story of escape.

Marisol and I were forced to move the human's heavy weapons like catapults and a huge battering ram they used to beat down the gates to an enemy's walled town.

"So, they made you help them fight battles against their own kind?" I was impressed that people trusted blue dragons to stay obedient right in the middle of a skirmish.

Believe it or not, there are some towns where humans fight among themselves. One such town is Rye, a small coastal port many, many miles south of Portville. The only approaches to the village are by sea or by land and the land approach is where they built a huge gate made of full-sized pine trees.

Yes, Marisol added. *We had to push the battering ram against that gate for a whole day. Our shoulders were rubbed raw before the gate finally gave way.*

"Why would you do such a thing?" I asked. "How could they make you—"

Venturo answered. *Much like they did with Skye and Caerulus, they held our child, Carina, hostage. They would kill her if we didn't comply.*

Carina, who was about the same size as Skye's middle child, leaned against her mother and made an odd little moaning sound.

I was stunned to realize how low humans would stoop to force their ways on dragons. I liked this family of dragons but it was disturbing to hear their story. I couldn't take my eyes off the floor of their cave for fear of meeting any of the dragons' gaze. For a few moments I just wanted to curl up and disappear.

But when I thought of their bravery to finally escape from the Big Barn all on their own one night, that helped ease my embarrassment. It was kind of funny that a ruckus broke out between two male dragons on the opposite side of the barn from this family's corral.

We still had our wing harnesses on, and we could only run after breaking out of our pen, Marisol said with pride. *After all, we had a lot of practice breaking through wooden enclosures.*

The two adult dragons made the funniest hollow gurgling sound deep in their chests. I guess that was more dragon laughter! Even Carina brightened up and added her higher pitched gurgling. It was good to see them in high spirits after going through such a terrible time.

Well, we must move on, Caerulus said with all seriousness as if no one had been laughing.

We excused ourselves and walked for a while in silence. I realized Skye hadn't finished her story about the Founders.

"So... What do these Founders think about all of you living near them?" I asked.

Not much, Skye said. *They call us Novis, which means the 'new ones.' It's a polite term for dragons without a clue. And it's true, we don't know how to fight. Most of us can't spit fire, though Caerulus and I have been lucky enough to have regained that knowledge as you know. We're sharing it with everyone in New Homestead and it's coming along well. The Founders call this whole land Septrion which roughly means 'northern regions.'*

Some blue dragons have brought along the smaller silver and gold dragons who were not so closely tied to their human handlers. Most of the silvers and golds are not too bright and easily lured to human service for the food and comfortable living quarters. That is, if you consider a wooden hut comfortable living. A few of the smaller dragons here have grown to prefer living in caves with their blue dragon families. The Founders have always had a number of smaller ones for courier service and as watch-dragons.

Caerulus leaned against his mate and looked intensely at me. *You must remember, that though this is a barren land away from the forests and farms of the hill country—and a hard land to live on—we're free. Probably not for long, which is why we must do more than only survive here. The Founders don't exactly agree. But no more about that for now.*

There Caerulus went again, not giving me the whole picture. I had a few answers, but mostly I just kept coming up with more questions.

SEVEN

Both Scary and Crazy

I found it interesting and a little scary to see so many dragons all in one place. They were scattered around in all kinds of caves and cliff dwellings, but their whole weyr wasn't much bigger than my village of Hilltop. I didn't count but I guessed there were about forty families, maybe two-hundred dragons of all kinds, though mostly blues.

Finished with my tour around New Homestead, we circled back toward Azure Den. As we approached a small mesa, Skye led us off the main track up a rocky trail that snaked among rocks and dirt that had rolled off the top of the mesa.

A few feet up the trail, we came to the foot of the sandstone cliffs where a tall, narrow cleft rose. It was nearly pitch dark inside except for a slender blade of light dozens of feet above our heads. Stepping inside the cleft, we came to a splinter-shaped rock jammed between the cliffs blocking our way.

Caerulus reached out and gripped the edge of the towering rock with his claws and slid it aside revealing a passageway. Beyond that was a large area surrounded by high cliff walls. All around the oblong patch of sand and rock that formed the floor of the enclosure, clusters of small wooden huts sheltered entrances to caves no taller than me. A wild cackling and high-pitched whining filled the enclosure as more than twenty gold and silver dragons streamed out of the caves. Most ran on the ground, a few flew out but quickly landed.

Seeing the big blues and little old me, the noise stopped like an interrupted nightmare. Caerulus quickly closed the passage behind us.

My skin crawled as if sharp claws were drawing winding lines all over my body while these dragons, smaller than blues, gathered around us a little too close for comfort and stared. Mostly at me.

"So, looks like you got yourself a nice little herd of golds and silvers, here, in this unusual corral." I said, trying to sound lighthearted.

Not so nice, but definitely a herd, Caerulus grumbled.

True, Skye added, *but they're coming along. All of these came voluntarily with a number of blue dragon families who escaped. These golds and silvers weren't fully trained by the humans so we have mostly broken them of bad habits learned from the humans. Come on, take a look up close.*

I edged toward a small group of golds who nervously wandered around on the sand, leaving trails with their feet that looked like a riot of snake tracks.

"Yeah, interesting," I said. I really didn't want to spend time around them, but I also didn't want to seem like I was scared of these beasts. The sight of them brought back the aerial battle Skye and Caerulus fought against a group of golds riding on silvers. That battle threatened to end our escape from the Big Barn when they attacked us in the hills north of Portville.

I heard muttering sounds, not like talking but more like the noise of restless dogs and nervous livestock. Their own versions of dragon language? I couldn't be sure.

As I watched these smaller dragons up close for the first time, I came to the conclusion they were pretty dumb compared to the blues. The silvers were like flying horses as they stomped back and forth and the golds resembled cranky, skittish dogs. Back when Skye and I hid in the dragon caves near Hilltop, the golds especially scared me. Like a hungry pack of wolves.

Among this bunch there was this one silver, clearly the largest one of the bunch, who didn't move, but stared at me pointedly. The rest avoided eye contact as if I were a mad dog, but that big silver had no such reluctance to engage my attention. After a long, uneasy time, I looked away and tried to make light of the menagerie.

"So, this is quite a group. I suppose you have plans for them, too?"

In time, young man, in time. And with that Caerulus didn't say another word. Skye acted as if she didn't even hear my comment when she pointed to another tall opening opposite where we entered the enclosure. This time she slid aside a rock blocking our exit so we could pass through. She immediately closed it behind us.

This is part of a tunnel system, some of it natural, some of it we have formed to connect the seven hills of New Homestead so that we wouldn't have to move about in the open, if necessary, Skye explained.

Heading back through the passage to an exit near Skye's family cave, I thought it was time to bring up the one subject on my mind.

"So, how can I help?" I asked. "I mean, right away. Like you said, I could hunt and cook to improve the meals. Maybe everyone would have more energy and enthusiasm if they ate better. Not that I know what's best for dragons, but if we put our heads together, we can figure it out."

I told you that's not why we brought you here. That will be fine for later, but we have more important matters to deal with now, Caerulus insisted.

I thought, At last! They're going to train me to be a warrior so I can fight the people treating the dragons so badly. But, when he went on, I lost heart.

We need to know what's going on with humans, especially the dragon train owners and the leaders in Portville. They must know we're out here somewhere but the openness and harshness of this land makes it difficult for them to sneak their way into this place and survive long enough to attack without us knowing in advance. Yet, they must be planning something. We can't simply fly over to find out. And it's hard for a blue dragon to slip in and out of the bigger towns where so many humans live.

Skye added, *It's too quiet. Some of the recent escaped dragons say the talk among the humans shows they're fearful of dragons who are free. Rumors of more blue dragons leaving the human lands have spread. They will come and it won't be long before they do.*

"Well, what about the silvers and golds?" I said. "The only ones I've seen, except for those back there in that tight little opening, are serving the human army. You remember that, Skye, when we hid from them in your old family cave. There might still be a few smaller dragons out on the Nulland Plains to herd cattle and chase off predators. Maybe a few are even wild. They might make good spies for us since people expect them to be trained to serve humans, not fellow dragons.

"Of course, those who have been trained by humans—I don't know," I said. "A long time ago, my father went to a village on the Nulland Plains and tried to buy a small dragon to work on the farm. But when he saw how they were treated by their human owners, it made him mad. He couldn't see himself having to treat a silver dragon that way and, I don't know, he never explained it, but I think he didn't want to deal with a beast that only knew that kind of treatment."

Surprisingly, I got a little choked up. I swallowed the big knot stuck in my throat. "It's like the only time I knew him to get worked up about treating animals right. He always made fun of me and got mad when I felt sorry for animals."

It was silent for a few moments. I was afraid I may have insulted my dragon friends by referring to these silvers and golds as animals.

I managed to say, "I don't think of you two or the other blues as animals like these smaller dragons. But still, I can't help but think none of you should be treated the way you have in the past."

Though he didn't say anything, he gave me a slight nod with a gleam in his eye that showed Caerulus understood how I felt.

Of course, Skye's voice in my head said softly. *You can't have feelings for animals or blue dragons without someone having that kind of influence in your life. Maybe he didn't say much around you but he did love your mother.*

I hardly thought about that! My father did love my mother the way he kept her picture by his bed and all. But he made it hard for me to appreciate that because of the way he treated me a lot of times. I just never thought of him caring about other living beings or even people that way. At least not very much. Recently, there had been some good times. I began to feel a little bad about leaving him to join the dragons.

Maybe I should have talked to him, I don't know. I could have said *something* before I just took off. But he made me so mad. I guess that's what happens sometimes when people get cross ways with each other.

In any case, Caerulus broke the uncomfortable silence. *Silvers and golds are dragons, but as you saw back there, they are as different from intelligent blues as dogs and cows are different from people. You understand that don't you?*

I nodded.

So, they can't be much help spying on humans and telling us anything of use. We need someone with a head on their shoulders. A human boy could move about and ask questions without attracting much attention. And that's you.

"Look, I guess I like the fact you thought of me for this, but I'm *not* a boy any more. And I don't think I'll be too good at this. I don't know much about what goes on in the big towns. I'm just a farmer."

Skye dipped her head down close to me. Though I only heard her in my mind, I could tell it was a low voice. Very calm.

You're right, you're not a boy anymore but you certainly aren't 'just a farmer.' Your skills will prove valuable to us as we strive to improve our lives and the food we eat until we move back to our homes in the forests of the Uplands. But, right now, we need you as a spy. And yes, we're considering the role golds and silvers can play in our plans. All of it is critical to our hopes for full freedom, otherwise we'll spend generations here in the dust and bramble of this miserable desert.

Me, a spy? I still couldn't get my head around that idea. I barely knew what that meant other than a few foul comments Dad made about spies during the Dragon Wars. But he wasn't talking about spies for the dragons. He meant those guys who lived side-by-side with the soldiers and reported back to the commanders when some of the men complained too harshly about their leaders and, as they called it, "the stupidity of fighting dragons with hand weapons."

No, that wasn't for me. I came to do something like fight in battle or, I don't know, something else useful like Skye said. But spying?

"What I want to do is learn how to shoot a crossbow." When I said that, Skye pulled her head back up and eyed me carefully. I thought she might be getting angry with me.

I went on in the hopes I could at least convince her. "I almost got my head split open by that guy who came after me on the train. You know, the train you and I captured on the Nulland Plains. The more I've thought about it, the more I'd like to shoot bolts from that kind of weapon."

Caerulus swung his head back and forth and spewed out a thin but hot flame. *Blast it, boy—or as you prefer, Jaiden! We don't have crossbows. We can spit fire, fly, crush puny humans, claw, and tear flesh, but we can't do anything that requires using tiny hands and fingers like yours.*

For a long time, our size and power gave us an advantage over people. However, most of us never wanted to lord it over humanity, we only wanted to be left alone. It worked until people got too devious and began to devise tools and plan ways to tilt the balance of power their way. Now the things made by little human brains and hands have enslaved us and driven us to this miserable land of dirt, scrub brush, and too little water. In fact, what water we have comes out of the northern mountains not far from where humans live. If they realize that, they'll cut off the flow of water and we'll be sunk!

Skye leaned over me again. *Please. Give spying a chance. We know there is more we need to learn about the humans. We can train you to use your senses in ways you've never imagined. Both Caerulus and I have been around people and eavesdropped on their thoughts but, most important, we still need to know about their plans. You can do this great service for us.*

She paused for several moments. Even Caerulus didn't say anything to fill the gap of silence.

Finally, Skye said, *It's true we don't know how you can go into a town or among a garrison of soldiers and not arouse suspicion. That's up to you to figure out, since you've lived around your fellow humans. We know that scares you and if it doesn't now, it will. But you're a smart young man. The way you helped me and, later, my family... You can do it. I—no, we—know you're smart enough. We'll teach you all we know about how the human leaders are organized and what they think about us. But you need to find out whatever you can about their plans to invade us here in Septrion.*

I wanted to say something right back to them, kind of like how I sometimes flew off the handle and dared to talk back to my father. But I couldn't be that way with Skye or even with Caerulus who seemed like a cranky old horse with a bur under his saddle.

Up to that point, I'd gotten all worked up about not missing out on what I imagined would be a big adventure. To be a part of something bigger than me. Yeah, right, a dumb farmer who knew next to nothing about the big world beyond his dumpy little town. Shoot, I didn't know much about war, dragons, or the mysterious parts of my dad's life before I was born. Now this whole thing I thought I couldn't live without was spread out in front of me by two blue dragons and I realized I could get myself in a lot of trouble, maybe even slaughtered like a useless old hen.

Their plan for me seemed impossible, but as I looked into those copper-flecked eyes of hers, I saw both a familiar kindness and an unfamiliar desperation. She and her mate were so powerful, yet at that moment, they were the weak ones and I had the one power they needed to survive. Only if I would agree to spy to help the dragons' cause for freedom.

That seemed both scary and crazy to me!

EIGHT

A Council of Dragons

After a few weeks, spy training reminded me of when I sat in our little one room schoolhouse listening to old Mr. Pettifog going on and on about writing a description of... I don't remember what. It was always something we had to describe or explain how it worked or what we thought about a poem of the heroes of the Dragon Wars. Meanwhile, I'd look out the back door of the school room, if the weather was pleasant, and dreamed battling dragons who'd fly off in a panic from such a mighty warrior.

What dumb thinking on my part. For one thing, as a kid I didn't really think much about dragons except I had those occasional fantasies because they were such a mystery to me. But all this spy stuff still made me think I was missing out on my big chance to be a hero because I was stuck listening to Skye and Caerulus talk endlessly about all the things they learned about humans during their captivity.

The two taught me interesting things like how humans made cannons from this thing called iron ore—taken right out of the ground! Also, people mixed other strange minerals to produce a black powder which can explode when lit with fire. Now that, I'd like to see! Anyway, by lighting the black powder inside a cannon with a spark, the explosion can shoot heavy iron balls right out the open end of those long tubes. Our blacksmith in Hilltop sure didn't form anything like that with his forge and anvil! All he did was make horseshoes, fix broken hoes and things like that.

How the armies were organized and all the different ranks was boring. What I didn't expect was how mad I felt about my dad having to put up with all kinds of things. Like the highest commanders sitting on his horse atop of a hill overlooking a battle. Talk about a soft job! Meanwhile, most of the lowly pikemen ended up burned to a crisp before they had a chance to do something useful with their twelve-foot pikes and lances like breech the barriers to the dragon caves.

I don't know what Dad did in the war, but from the few times he complained about it—of course, he didn't go into any details—the whole thing for him didn't seem that exciting. Like him, I didn't find any of that interesting. Not even the things Skye told me about the whole dragon train system.

Training *how* to fight would have been very exciting, but Caerulus had no intention of preparing me for war. On top of that, Skye didn't know much about it since the wars and her family's capture happened before she grew up.

Finally, the very morning I was going to tell Caerulus I didn't want to hear any more about government or the train business, Skye broke into my thoughts with a surprise.

We have not talked very much about the dragons who live here. We've kept you away from the others because we wanted you to be ready to help our cause before they had a chance to complain about a human among us.

"Really? The dragons I've met haven't said much about me."

That was at our request, Caerulus said. *We assured our Weyr leaders about you by telling them the story of how you and the other boys at the Big Barn helped us escape. Even at that, many would suspect your intentions if we had taken you before the entire Septrion Council. Now that time has come. We want to show them what you can do.*

"I guess I hadn't thought that much beyond all the crud you've thrown at me."

'Crud?' What's this crud? Caerulus turned to Skye.

It's his way of saying 'dragon manure.'

Caerulus narrowed his eyes and took a deep breath ready to burn me like I was rearing back to launch a javelin right through his throat. I swear I heard a grinding sound deep in his throat as he prepared to belch sulfur and torch me.

Skye leaned toward her mate and gently wrapped her neck once around his neck. *Now, calm down, dear one. He has a good point. He's had to take in many things you know he's not really interested in. It's time for the Council to see him at his best and not as a beaten down young man who's tired of us and our endless prattle about the humans. He wants to help and we've kept him from being useful long enough. Imagine how our own youngsters would tire of all this going on and on.*

Caerulus slowly released all of the air from his vast lungs. He looked a little deflated but his eyes still sparkled with fire. *My love, you are right. This is highly important to me, to all of us. He's our best hope but he has to understand that.*

He does, but he's young and tired of our talk-talk-talk. Let's go now, the Council will start very soon.

And that was that.

Since Skye didn't want to waste time while I buckled her leather strap back on for a short flight, I gripped a couple of the spines on Skye's back instead. She took off gently, flying at a slow pace a few feet off the ground. I was glad she didn't want me to lose my grip, otherwise all my training would have been for nothing if I ended up plastered into the sand and rock below.

We flew beyond the few hills where the Novis lived. We passed over an unfamiliar landscape streaked with red and brown sand as we crossed a deep canyon where a thin stream, called Rio Roho, twisted its way along its bottom, flowing northward from the southern mountains. The other side of the canyon was cluttered with those tall, flat-topped hills the dragons called mesas. I imagined it would be nearly the same to look down on the big tall buildings of Portville. Finally, we approached a circular open area at the top of a single narrow mesa that towered over all the rest.

As we landed, I saw two groups of dragons massed together around a pile of rocks at the center. They milled about while a few more flew onto the mesa. On the central pile of rocks, the biggest blue dragon I had ever seen fully extended his wings like a humongous eagle. He made Caerulus look like a sparrow in comparison.

The two hordes of dragons, mostly blues with a few silvers underfoot and a smattering of golds flitting about like hummingbirds, gave up a loud roar. The huge dragon flapped his wings stirring up two dust devils that danced through the crowd. When one of the whirlwinds reached me, it clawed at my skin like a thousand needles as it passed, leaving me with a mouth full of gritty sand.

The inside of my head filled with a voice like thunder.

Weyrs of Septrion, I, Hellmuth of the Founders, call this Council to order. Be silent and attend to the matters at hand!

Hellmuth, huh? No doubt existed in my mind whose voice rattled the rocks. Either his parents knew something about his future or he was named once he made his personality known. Hellmuth had to be the Biggest and Baddest Demon from Hell.

Actually, the legends say his original name is unknown, and his father gave him 'Hellmuth' as a nickname years later. Whether it was constant dust ups with childhood rivals or fighting the human armies in his early years as an attack dragon, Hellmuth seemed quite appropriate.

"Skye, you're reading my thoughts again!"

Sorry, but your mind 'spoke' those words, loud and clear.

"Speaking of loud, the Big Guy makes more noise than a summer thunderstorm."

Right then that thunderstorm blasted across the mesatop. *Silence! I hear voices speaking without permission. I demand silence and undivided attention.*

Hellmuth's eyes scanned the multitude like a razor cutting off heads and stopped on Skye and Caerulus. I slipped behind them and peeked around Skye's legs to watch Hellmuth. Both bowed their heads. I sensed an overwhelming wave of fear pass over me as they kept their heads low against their chests.

Yikes. There was no doubt the Big Blue Guy up front was not going to suffer any lack of attention or messing around from the crowd. Fortunately, Hellmuth gave a quick nod of his head and his gaze moved on as Skye and her mate released a sigh sounding like the last gust of passing squall.

"Why didn't old Hellmuth just fry me right here and now?" I whispered frantically.

Skye's words came to me in such a small voice that I wasn't sure if I imagined them rather than "heard" anything at all. *We assured him we would explain your presence at his council when it pleased him to grant us and you permission to speak. Now be quiet!*

"Why did you say anything to him? He scares the life out of me! Besides, I didn't even hear you talking to him."

Caerulus said, *There is a way dragons can speak to each other privately, like the difference you humans make when you whisper something to another person as others stand around speaking out loud. Also, we used dragon language which is not based on human words like we use with you. It's like the thoughts you have that aren't in words, more like emotions, images in your mind, intentions for which there are no words.*

"I've been wondering about that because I've sensed some weird things being exchanged between you two, so I figured it was dragon language.

Never mind that, Skye interrupted, her voice fearful. *Hellmuth has ascended to the top of the rock pile. He is ready to speak and if he tries, he can hear even human whispers and quiet dragon language. Silence!*

I clammed up as ideas swirled around in my head trying to think how I could quietly disappear so I wouldn't have to speak to Hellmuth or the Council. I sure wasn't prepared to speak in front of a big herd of dragons. Or "weyrs" as they would put it. What to do, what to do?

The next hour consisted of Hellmuth spouting a series of roars and shrieks that I couldn't explain in mere words. I thought my heart was going to jump out of my chest as I heard not only Hellmuth's carrying-on but equally creepy responses from the horde of dragons.

Finally, it got so quiet, I could hear the creaking of dragon scales as those around me shifted their positions leaving my two dragon friends and me encircled. Hellmuth came off the pile of rocks and stomped over to us, making the ground shake so much I got woozy from the sensation the earth was going to open up and swallow me.

Now, what is the reason for bringing a scurvy human in our midst?

Caerulus gathered himself and stood tall on his claws and held his head high with his neck stretched upward before he spoke.

As I have proposed to our weyr leader, I want the Council and you, our Great Leader, to consider making use of humans who are sympathetic to our cause of freedom. I present to you Jaiden, the major instigator who secured our escape from the Big Barn of Train Dragons in the human city of Portville. He and others can offer a great service to us. Please allow him to talk and answer your questions.

And with that, Caerulus and Skye faced me as all eyes on the mesa turned in my direction. Why did Caerulus and Skye only tell me *after* we got here that I had to do this? I still had no idea what to say, but I had to do something or get burned to a crisp in the next few moments.

"I wanted to, uh, your eminence or whatever your title is, um, Mr. Hellmuth—"

Simply Hellmuth is enough. Only self-centered little insects calling themselves humans waste words with titles like Eminence, and Your Highness. Speak! I'm getting tired of hearing your useless prattle.

No pressure.

I opened my mouth and prayed to all the Angels in Heaven that something making sense would come out of my mouth if I even had enough breath to make a sound.

"I know I don't have the size, power, or talent like—uh, your ability to spit fire, and to—you know—fly. But I'm small and can be tricky most like any human who can, pardon the expression, overpower dragons by using tools, weapons, and working together.

"Really, I don't like some of the things people do, but together, we seem to be pretty dangerous if we want to be, that's for sure. But a lot, at least, enough people do and so, here we are with people all over the place using dragons to pull trains, do farm work, and I think there are some who even help fight other dragons. But... I don't like that. I think dragons have a right—"

Hellmuth reared back his head and roared, *You're telling us what we already know! Tell me something I don't know. Tell me what you think you can do to help us. Or why are you among us? Are you really here to help the humans know more about us?*

"No, no, I'm sorry. I'm trying to think. I had no idea..." I had to take a deep breath because my vision was starting to cloud up and the world around me was turning dark. "Give me a minute."

I forced my lungs to fill with air and then slowly spew it out. Finally, I felt a little better. My vision cleared.

"I think I'm all right now. Anyway, because I'm a human I can go among people and find out what they're planning. What they know about this place, Septrion, and about you, and how many are here. I'm sure they want to have a good idea how this whole place is laid out and what dragons are willing to do to stay free.

"So, I can turn the tables on them and find out what *they* intend. I'm old enough, so I can volunteer to do something to supposedly help the human cause. But I have to be careful. I don't want to be one of their soldiers, but maybe something else to support their cause. Then I can learn more about their plans.

"If I get information back to you on a lot of things like that, you'll know what to do. What to look for. Who knows, you may all have to move from here to some other place they don't expect or somewhere they can't go without a lot of trouble. Like I said, you can fly, spit fire, and so on..."

My brain was empty. I couldn't even think of nonsense just to keep talking. I took another deep breath and dared raise my focus from the Big Guy's shadow to look him in the eye. Can a look kill someone? Looking into those piercing eyes, feeling the turmoil behind them, yet with no idea what he was thinking, I would say, "Yes, his look could kill a whole army."

Maybe that's how the dragons can win their freedom, just have Hellmuth stare the humans down. But I didn't think it was a good idea to voice that right at the moment!

I heard a low-toned rumbling from the horde of dragons. It didn't sound friendly.

Sharp-toned voices cut into my mind, each one piling on top of each other. Some of the voices I understood.

Does this human manure think we should believe he can go among his own kind without them knowing he's either an idiot or a traitor to their cause? Those of us who've spent our lives fighting and now have to hide from filthy people know better!

He's a child, not a man. What can he do or learn from wandering among his devious elders? Nothing! I've been around long enough to know. He will get caught and do harm to our cause.

Yes, then they'll know we're up to something and they'll storm their trains to the end of their lines and swarm across our free lands like locust! It's what I've been saying all along—

You are right! I've seen how the sneaky humans operate. They will capture him and squeeze everything from him about us. He's only a scolded child. A very foolish and stupid—

Another voice, with a different tone cut through the noise. *Fools! Can't you see that he is our best chance to insure our freedom! I've lived among them as one of their slaves. It won't be easy but we can't fight them like the Founders did in the old days. Look what happened. Right now, we can't go among people except as their servants and beasts of burden.*

And another voice said, *Exactly. Some of us have lived around people, in fact, a few have been born and trained under their whips and lances. We can't fight like you old timers did. Those glorious days are gone. We have to do something different. Who will suspect a boy working for our cause?*

As the din of thoughts increased in volume and intensity, I realized those who believed I had a chance to help came from close around me. Of course, I still didn't like being called a boy! The old warriors from the Dragon Wars were probably right. I was a lost cause.

A familiar voice cut into my thoughts. *It is as you have realized. The Novis think a new way is needed. The old ones are very wise and experienced in war, but they can't admit that their old ways of fighting failed, and we are too few to go to war like that again.*

It was Skye. Her voice reassuring and reaching into my core just like she did from the beginning as she lay suffering on the tracks when I first saw her. She and her mate were not giving up on me, but what about Hellmuth? He was obviously the leader, though the older dragons didn't seem to be bashful about speaking their minds with or without his permission.

Then, I swear I heard the Big Blue leader clear his throat.

All fell silent.

He must have said something in dragon language because the sudden quiet didn't happen by accident.

He looked down at me, his eyes intense. This is it. He was going to fry me right then.

He didn't.

The boy makes sense. I've been listening to Caerulus and Skye's thoughts during his rambling little speech. I like their ideas. He raised his head and scanned the two hordes of dragons that were beyond my limited vantage point next to my two protectors.

And of course, my compatriots of the Dragon Wars, I've heard you as well. I feel the same. Crush the devil humans with our claws and fire. But—

I sensed hundreds of pairs of lungs suddenly stop breathing. Hellmuth slowly raised his gaze to the Heavens. After a long pause, his expression slowly melted from a scary intensity beyond description to something more like a comrade as he lowered his head to me.

I'm willing to allow you to give this plan a try. I've searched your mind while you spoke, Jaiden, and I see you still need some skills, especially survival and fighting skills.

Without intending to, I said, "Yes, sir. I'd like to learn how to use a crossbow—"

Never mind that. I mean you need to learn the cunning use of your body to defend and attack in ways that your kind won't expect of someone without a weapon. If you're carrying a crossbow without being a trained soldier or enforcer of some kind, you will arouse suspicion.

For one thing, you will learn to be a rider. You'll have a silver dragon to train with and who will travel with you as if he's your personal beast. Caerulus and Skye can attend to the details.

That's all for now. I don't entirely like this idea, yet I have spoken. What does the Council say?

The air filled with a sound like a mass of violent thunderstorms approaching. Strangely enough, it sounded both like celebration and anger.

But I'm pretty sure that was a "yes" from the Council. For now.

Whether celebration or angry frustration, I had to get away from the commotion. Someone like me would quickly get squashed like a cockroach if I stayed in that crowd, so I darted among the Novis' feet, under their vast bellies, and found myself in the open quickly enough. In my mind, I sensed a nod of approval from Skye. She understood.

I walked toward the edge of the mesa and looked out across the dusty red landscape wondering how in the world and all that's good and true, was I going to fulfill this mission. A job approved by the big ol' Hellmuth no less. What did I do to myself?

The long shadows of early morning had grown shorter as the bright sun washed out the more brilliant colors of the mesas and tortured hills. Back home in Hilltop, all the hills were covered in shades of green whether with wild mountain laurel and flowers or crops where we cultivated the land. In winter, the land was mostly brown with a tinge of green from the laurel bushes that never lost their dark green leaves for the season.

But here, it was dirt and rock with a few scrappy bushes the dragons called sage. Many of the hills and mesas had high cliffs made of sandstone and hard rock. Some of the cliffs looked like a layer cake of different flavors with their colors of yellow, brown, red, white, and gray. Strange place, more like a dream than real.

Soon I heard big feet and claws scratching across the gravel behind me.

Ready to cross back over the canyon to New Homestead? Skye said.

"Yeah. It's not quite like my little home on the farm with Dad, but it's home for now."

I latched on to a couple of spines on Skye's back and we made our way back to Azure Den with Caerulus following. She dropped me off and seemed to sense I needed to be alone to think.

She only said, *Don't wander too far.*

Skye and Caerulus went into their cave, and I heard the excited chattering of their young ones. I still hadn't spent any time with them to get reacquainted. I really liked those crazy little dragons.

Right then I headed west for several minutes, thinking in circles.

I would have to take things one step at a time to make sense out of it. Only one thought kept coming back at me. Maybe I should go back home, ask Dad for forgiveness and not tell him a gal-durned thing about all this dragon business. He wouldn't believe me anyway and he'd only get madder than usual.

That might be better than living my life as a spy. It was getting too big for me to handle.

Right at that moment, I heard the whistling of dragon wings and excited chirps.

Three young dragons flew right at me at top speed. I threw myself face first into the fine dust and coarse sand. My mouth was full of grit and dried weeds.

I heard dragon feet settle hard on the ground and then running feet, claws kicking up rocks and torn twigs from the dried-out bushes.

Jaiden! Jaiden! Jaiden! Three high-pitched voices filled my brain so much that I gripped the sides of my head to keep it from exploding.

When they reached me, Skye and Caerulus' three youngsters picked me up and took turns pushing against me and wrapping their necks around my middle, greeting me with their version of cuddling and hugging.

All three were taller and more filled out than the last time I saw them. Already, the oldest son, Baldric, was about three feet taller than me and almost as big as a full-grown heifer. The middle child, Deryn, pushed against me with real strength though she was only a little smaller than me, but much longer than I was tall.

The youngest, Jarmil, bumped against me like a playful pup, but now he was about as big as his sister had been a couple of years ago. Not only that, but he could push me over if he had half a mind to do so.

"How did you kids grow so much? Doesn't it take decades for you to get really big like your parents?"

But all they did was laugh—I think it was laughter—in a sing-song whistle that pierced my ears. Didn't matter to me, their enthusiasm and joy had all the healing power of a litter of puppies.

I quickly forgot my fears, regrets, and second thoughts. I think we must have played for over an hour while they chattered constantly about all kinds of adventures they'd had as they discovered curious and exciting things in this new land of dragons.

Oh well, tomorrow I could start training how to ride a silver. Today would be a time for fun and games.

NINE

After the Practice Session

Finally, the aches and pains of my first practice flying on that rat, silver dragon Trigger, worked themselves out as I wandered for quite a while by myself and remembered how I had gotten to this point. Going back to my father, coming with Skye to this land of free dragons, meeting other escaped blue dragons, and all the rest.

Hellmuth would not take no for an answer, and Caerulus was determined I measured up, but something had to be done about Trigger, like send him back to the corral in the tunnel and get someone more cooperative to be my, uhm, dragon horse or whatever he is.

When Caerulus introduced me to Trigger, I knew there was something about him I didn't like. Later, I remembered. He was the bigger silver who stared at me like I was a pile of manure when Caerulus and Skye took me through the tunnel to that hidden corral.

At first, it seemed like that scary ride on that silver's back made Caerulus mad at both Trigger and me. It was only later that Caerulus reassured me that Trigger was instructed to give me a scare so I would learn the value of hanging on tight and how to be ready when a silver had to move about and change directions quickly in an air battle. Fine. I said I would do my best. Still, I didn't like or trust that dad-blamed silver!

Anyway, right after Trigger scared me and before Caerulus explained what the silver was really trying to do, I had a lot to think about. So, I wandered aimlessly for quite a while when another silver flew over me in a rush to talk to Skye and Caerulus. Whatever news that other silver brought, it caused the two blues to get upset about something to do with their children. They consoled each other for a while after twisting their necks around each other. Finally, the pair flew away in the direction of their home, Azure Den.

After too much self-pity about events over the last several days, I realized there was only one thing for me to do. I also headed back to Azure Den, hoping to find out what happened to their young ones.

As I walked, my thoughts kept churning. I know I shouldn't have stirred things up about "Manure Breath"— my new preferred name for Trigger—which annoyed Caerulus because I needed him as well as Skye on my side so I could get a different silver to ride.

"Manure Breath"? Really? An irate dragon voice cut right through my thoughts. A voice sounding a lot like Caerulus.

I looked around. Is he back here, already? Or was this his own ability to read my thoughts at long distances? It was bad enough Skye could eavesdrop on my thoughts, but Caerulus?

"You weren't supposed to hear that," I said to the empty flat lands around me. "I really wish you dragons wouldn't interfere in my thoughts. It's not that I don't trust you any less than Skye, but it's kind of creepy no matter who does it." I spun around looking for him. "Where are you?"

Your little problems with Trigger, a reckless silver who was merely following orders, is not important. Something terrible has happened.

Suddenly a strong wind blasted me from behind as the sound of dragon wings flailing against a granite wall filled my ears. The sunlight winked out as a gigantic shadow flew over my head. It was Caerulus flying extremely low to the ground, his wing tips kicking up sand and shredding sage bushes, sending them into the air like so much dead grass.

"What in Hades' name—?" I ran after him as if I could actually catch up.

As he flew over me, a strong emotion radiated through me like a bonfire. It was, I don't know, despair? That didn't make sense but it was so strong, it scared me. My heart pounded in my chest as if I feared Caerulus would turn and beat me into the desert sand. So why was I running *to* him and not *away?*

No idea, but the impulse was stronger than the desire to escape.

He glided over a low hill and disappeared as if the bleak land swallowed him whole. I ran to the top of the hill and saw him spread out, face down in a narrow arroyo between two sand hills. I stopped, leery that he planned to fry me with a mighty blast of fire.

I heard only deep, ragged breaths like a child trying to resist crying. Caerulus, the big blue dragon crying? Not possible. At least I didn't think so. I dared to make a noise clearing my throat.

No reaction from him.

Taking this as a sign to retreat as softly as possible, I turned and heard an odd dragon sound in my head that made my stomach turn. Discovered! But before I could break out running, Caerulus spoke.

They're gone! But don't be afraid of me. Don't leave. At first, we weren't really worried... We need to go back to Skye. At first, we had a wonderful time flying, singing, and enjoying each other on our way back to Azure Den so sure everything was all right. That young silver who came for us. He was scared something had happened to—

Trigger left after the practice session to help that silver watch our children. And Skye... She felt bad about how

Trigger tested you and wouldn't let it go in spite of my urging her to stay out of it.

But that doesn't matter anymore. The most terrible— There was a long pause as Caerulus face grimaced. He opened his mouth wide. Maybe to scream? It made my blood run cold to see him like this.

Finally, I heard his voice in my head like a harsh whisper. *After the young silver came to us... We returned to our cave while I was thinking maybe I shouldn't push it after arguing about you with her. No need to ruin it with my— Whatever you want to call it, 'Point of View.' Sometimes she's just not interested in what I think when it comes to you.*

Wow, Caerulus was going crazy right in front of me but what do I say? What is he talking about? But I had to say something because Caerulus just lay there paralyzed.

"Oh, well I appreciate her support, but maybe I should deal with Trigger—"

Quiet! The most tragic thing has happened. It's so hard to say.

The big blue twisted and flung his head so wildly he almost knocked me off the hill.

Our children are gone. Nowhere to be found. We looked. No one was around our cave. When Skye saw the children's empty nest, she knew they were gone. She screamed in a way that froze my heart.

I found footprints, human footprints, leading up to our cave. How could they have gotten in? It's broad daylight, yet I could tell by the way those wicked human tracks were twisted disturbing the sand. Long marks from our children's tails dragging along showed they took them by force!

"The youngsters? How's that possible?" I don't know how I even had breath left to say anything. "What could they—Great Creator! How!"

You should know, you've heard the tales told by Skye! I saw it every day in the Big Barn. Ropes, whips. There were at least nine to ten people who attacked. It would take at least four to get Baldric strung up, another three for Deryn, and one or two for little Jarmil. I don't know how they got that far into Septrion without being seen.

I followed their smelly tracks to Rio Roho just north of the human lands to the south before it heads down our canyon. They must have come on a northbound dragon train to the end of the line at the forests' edge, paddled down the Roho, and trekked through these hills along arroyos and canyons. Then while we were away from the cave and neighbors were out of sight, they attacked our children.

Maybe they created a diversion to the west to draw our neighbors away for a short time. I don't know. He stopped and twisted his body in frustration.

They must know something about our weyr and the layout of Septrion.

"Wasn't Trigger supposed to go back and watch them?"

Yes, that fool! And you think his games with you were bad? I ordered him to test you and give you a sense of what disaster could happen in battle. It was a little trick, don't blame him for that.

But this! He was supposed to relieve that younger silver, Thanos, who had been on duty the whole time inside the cave. They both fell asleep and allowed the children to be taken. How could that happen?

Thanos hasn't been fully trained but at least when he woke up, he knew enough to come tell us they were gone. Trigger is supposed to have the keenest hearing and the strongest awareness when people are nearby. He grew up around humans! He's supposed to hate them!

He pulled himself up and shook the sand off his body. He peered at me sideways and it was obvious. The fire had gone out of his eyes and his huge head drooped in a way that made me sadder than his news.

I wanted to track those filthy humans all the way back into their foul forests but I couldn't bear to leave Skye. Yet... I have to, but she's... She's inconsolable and I shouldn't be here now. But instead of tracking the human scum, she insisted that I find you first and bring you back. I promised her I would. She said you can help... to find the children.

"Me? What could I do?" All the air in my lungs just came out in a single big sigh. "I mean, look, I'm crazy about those kids but I have no clue what to do. I'm hardly a human fighter much less a blue dragon like you."

She has something in mind but was too upset to explain. She insisted you come.

Now!

TEN

Treacherous Water

Azure Den had plenty of room for two full-grown blues and their three little ones. But not the crowd of blues that filled the cave and spilled outside on the hardened dirt after the news had spread about the abduction of Skye and Caerulus' children. I fought my way to the entrance after I dismounted Caerulus several yards away. It was quite a squeeze through a thick forest of dragon legs and swinging tails as the horde milled around like a brood of chickens avoiding a fox.

Not only that, but the ride from the practice field to the den was a white-knuckle experience. Caerulus flew twice as fast as Skye ever had. Also, he didn't seem to care whether or not I could hang off his side gripping a couple of his spines. Where was a nice wide strap to hold onto when I needed it?

I made my way to the center of the crowded cave, noisy with throaty sounds of dragon language, and found Skye lying down on her stomach surrounded by some of the blue dragons I had met on our walkabout: the two brothers Lucas and Owyn, the family of Venturo, Marisol, and Carina, and others I hadn't met before. Marisol and Carina were snuggled up on either side of Skye as if to keep her upright.

Skye uttered a sound I never wanted to hear again. Something like a cry of despair combined with a growl of rage. Not only did it hurt my ears but it vibrated my stomach so much I thought I was going to throw up.

Against a back wall was a huddle of somewhat bigger and older blues clad with rougher skin than the others—Founders. Caerulus had just joined them as they tightened the huddle to enclose him. I headed over to this group of grumbling giants and nearly got crushed by an even bigger, rugged blue coming up behind me. Hellmuth.

What do we know about how this happened? Hellmuth demanded. The entire cramped den suddenly became quiet as a tomb. He turned and scanned the mob. *When I want to ask any of you a question, I'll face you. Tend to our sister,*

Skye, and don't concern yourself with my conversation with Caerulus and these comrades.

Every dragon head turned away and, slowly, whispers started up, then murmurs, and finally soft grunting. Since I was nearly invisible in this congregation of giants, I worked my way to Caerulus for protection. I don't know if he saw me, but I got a piercing gaze from Hellmuth for a long enough time that he could have melted me like a drooping candle. Then he gave me the slightest nod and I was able to breathe again.

Hellmuth turned his attention to Caerulus. *Do I need to repeat myself?*

No, of course not, Caerulus said, a little irritated. *I'm sorry if I sound impatient but this should have never happened. I left this silver, Thanos, to watch our children.* Caerulus pointed with his snout to a silver dragon who twitched and swayed at his feet. *Step forward and explain to Hellmuth what happened.*

The silver slithered forward and turned in the direction of Hellmuth but never made eye contact with the blue leader. I heard a small, wispy voice in my head. Where did that come from? I looked at the cowering silver dragon. Something in his eyes seemed to tell me it was him! I didn't think about silvers talking into my head like the blue dragons could, but the way his head nodded and darted about, it seemed to follow the faint words I was hearing. The silver slithered forward and turned in the direction of Hellmuth but never made eye contact with the blue leader. I heard a small, wispy voice in my head. Where did that come from? I looked at the cowering silver dragon. Something in his eyes seemed to tell me it was him! I didn't think about silvers talking into my head like the blue dragons could, but the way his head nodded and darted about, it seemed to follow the faint words I heard. I concentrated as hard as I could so I could understand him.

Then his scratchy sounding words became clearer.

Caeru tell me. Watch young ones. I not say no, but scared something happen. Thanos only small silver, not big blue. Young blues nice but jump a lot. Noisy. I chase them, but they faster. Kept them near cave, so all good. Long time. Trigger come. Help Thanos. That good. Trigger faster than young ones. Good.

At that point, Thanos shivered as if a cold wind from the east blew through the overcrowded and damp cavern.

Well? Hellmuth grumbled.

Not well. Bad. Trigger and Thanos get hot... dry, chasing young ones playing. Drink water. There. Thanos pointed to a wide basin formed in the sandstone of the floor near the wall behind the youngsters' nest. *Water nice. Cool. Trigger and Thanos feel better. Go outside. Watch over young ones. Thanos tired chasing young blues, lay down, close eyes. Trigger near. Trigger watch young ones. Thanos...*

He stopped and swallowed hard. He darted his head back and forth as if looking for a way to escape.

Go on, Caerulus thundered. Thanos fidgeted but said nothing. Caerulus turned to Hellmuth. *Beg your pardon, but let me finish his story. Trigger didn't last much longer than this sniveling fool and also lay down to nap. I can't understand how stupid they are! Even if our children were doing no more than playing, bad things could happen if no one with any sense is around to keep them out of trouble.*

We blues are sometimes too smart and curious for our own good as it is, but children? They don't understand what trouble is until they find it. Then it's too late.

Of course, I understand, Hellmuth said in a voice gentler than I ever would've imagined from the giant, scary leader.

This whole thing was against my better judgement, Caerulus continued, *but Trigger had said Thanos seemed like he understood better than any of the other mob of silvers who came along with escaped Novis. None joined Skye and me, although I was familiar with them when they worked in the Big Barn where we were held as captive train dragons in Portville. Other dragons have made friends with silvers before they were perverted by the humans who trained and tempted them with abundant food and nice living quarters. In fact, Trigger said Thanos had grown up with him. I just don't understand this foolishness. I thought I could trust Trigger. He's the one who should have known better.*

Bring Trigger, Hellmuth roared. Venturo left the group and went off to a back room in the den. He returned, pushing Trigger ahead of him with hard hits from his snout. Trigger scampered as quickly as he could, but tripped and fell at Caerulus and Hellmuth's feet. Thanos took several backward steps to hide in the shadows.

Without thinking, I made eye contact with Trigger and gave him the worst evil eye I've ever given. I didn't care that he was bigger than I was. The way he treated me and his foolish behavior watching over the young blues burned me up with anger. And to think all this time he could have talked to me and understood me just made me even madder.

He quickly dropped his gaze and stared at the sandy floor.

Explain yourself, Hellmuth said in an icy voice.

Trigger glanced up no higher than the big leader's knees. *I help Thanos take care young ones. Watch. Chase. Keep them safe. Thanos small, not smart. Trigger help, not hurt. Young ones run, yell, poke Trigger. Thanos just laugh. But Trigger help. Got tired. Thirsty. Drink water. Taste good. Taste not right, but good. Soon Thanos sleep. Stupid Thanos. Soon Trigger tired. Just close eyes. Not sleep. But... I sleep long, long time. Wake up. Thanos gone. Young blues gone. Trigger crazy. Scared. Look all round. No young ones! Caerulus, Skye come. Get mad. Yell. Hurt Trigger. Thanos gone. I talk, but Caerulus want kill Trigger. I run. Caerulus catch Trigger. Hit and burn but not kill. Young ones gone. Not know where. Please, Trigger sad. Scared.*

Caerulus twisted, swinging his tail. If Venturo hadn't been right next to him, I swear he would have knocked Trigger down and burned him to a crisp right in front of everyone.

Can't say I blamed him.

Thanos reappeared out of the shadows behind the blues in the huddle. He stepped closer to Hellmuth.

First, water good. Trigger come. Then water taste not right. But Thanos thirsty. Thanos drink. Tired. Long time watch young ones. Sleep. Trigger watch young ones. Good. But Thanos wake, find Trigger asleep. Young ones gone. Look, look, look. No young ones! Scared Thanos. Fly to Caeru. Tell Caeru young ones gone. Trigger sleep. Caeru, Skye come, yell, cry. Thanos feel bad. Stupid. Trigger sleep. Thanos try. Trigger stupid too. But Thanos try. Try. Try.

Hellmuth looked at the writhing silver and just shook his head the same way my dad would when I did something so stupid, he couldn't believe any human could be that dense. Those were the few times I didn't get punished because he believed I was hopeless. Thanos must have thought the same thing, because he retreated to the shadows without flinching. I can't be sure of what Hellmuth and Thanos thought, but I recognized what I saw going on between the big blue leader and the fearful silver.

I moved away from the huddle of male blue dragons because I was afraid I could get stomped or burned too, if they all cut loose on Trigger and Thanos. I ran out into the cool outdoor air and sat on a rock away from the commotion.

That evening with everyone gone except Hellmuth, Marisol and Carina stayed with Skye. I made my way back into Azure Den when Caerulus, seeming to hide in the deep shadows of the cave, came out and looked at me blankly. He and the blue leader moved quietly outside and squat on a wide, flat stone watching the bright red and orange clouds streak across the dying glow of sunset. I joined them.

Caerulus released a sigh that sounded like a torrential wind.

I don't know what to believe, he said. *But we know the humans came and took our children. The evidence is clear in the tracks those bandits left in the sand as they dragged* them off. *To get here, they must have worked their way north looking for places where dragons could establish family caves until they got lucky and found ours. To our bad luck!*

He continued. *They must have seen our young blues with either one or both silvers and put something in the water to make the silvers sleep. Any human who has worked in a dragon barn, especially the Big Barn in Portville, will know how limited silvers are but that they will sometimes also serve blue dragons just like humans work for the rich as servants.*

Hellmuth said, *How would the humans know to bring poison?*

They are a clever and devious bunch. You fought them, you know how they quickly learned how to win battles and capture dragons alive. Well, Skye and the rest of us Novis lived under their rule. They do things with plants and the minerals of the earth to create brews that can make an enemy sick or die. Why not cause a silver to fall asleep as well?

The blue leader grunted. *Why didn't they simply kill the silvers and your children? Why go to this trouble and take such a risk to sneak into Septrion for such a pointless mission?*

Because they want to antagonize us and turn us against each other. They want to draw us out of this land into their hands... at least our young ones and turn them into slaves, too. They aren't like you and the Founders. You're brave and ferocious. You confront your enemies directly in a heroic battle of the strong and brave. Not sneaky and underhanded. Skye's family was captured by filthy humans dressed as a wolf pack.

Hellmuth laughed, but the tone of his laugh didn't sound like he thought something was funny. It was the laugh of one who has been outsmarted, made to feel foolish. *They are a curse on the land. There were some brave among them, but those who were brave died, burned by dragon fire. The others ran us out of the forest lands, rich with food and comforts, so we ended up in this harsh place. Now they seek to lure us to defeat. Again!*

So, that's it, Caerulus said. *Our dumb silvers were made to be fools to show us they know where we live and they're ready to chase us away. Of course, they probably hope we kill our silvers and golds because now we should suspect them of working with the humans.*

Hellmuth growled. *I never wanted those little slimy things underfoot. Sure, they're dragons, but stupid enough to betray us for a full belly and a warm place to sleep.*

I know, but Trigger and Thanos were corral workers in the Big Barn. I knew them pretty well. Apparently, they were obstinate with the humans, not following orders, not cooperating. Young, poor humans are used to doing the dirty work of caring for blue dragons. Cleaning up after us, feeding us, repairing the corrals and barns. And keeping us retrained. But I could see those two silvers were not the servants of people, so they were confined with us and forced to do hard labor. Humans threatened them with a brutal death as well as giving them a taste of the whip. I made friends with Trigger and Thanos, and when they escaped a few weeks after Skye and I left, I took them on. Trigger is especially smart and capable. The only thing

Skye could say to me tonight was that she didn't blame the silvers. But as for me, now... I don't know.

Kill them and be done, Hellmuth said flatly.

I would but they may prove useful if I can be sure they don't act stupid again!

Well, that was certainly an interesting conversation between Caerulus and Hellmuth. I didn't realize what the silvers and golds were really like since my dad didn't say much except how he felt sorry for the silver he almost bought to use on the farm. Right now, though, I didn't feel a bit sorry for those two slippery demons. I wouldn't trust them to catch flies with their mouths. And I certainly wouldn't trust them with anything to do with the safety of children and freedom for dragons in Septrion.

There was a long silence as the three of us watched the stars come out and begin their eternal twinkling. I needed to forget underhanded silver dragons and my friends' loss of their children, so I wondered about the stars instead. Are they just some kind of little fires stuck way up in the sky? I didn't realize how high until the day before when Skye took me into the clouds. How much higher were the stars?

Finally, I cleared my throat and asked, "So what's next? What about Baldric, Deryn, and Jarmil?"

The heads of the two blue dragons turned and looked down at me. Even in the dim starlight I could tell by their blank facial expressions that they had forgotten I existed.

Tomorrow, the dragons of Septrion organize to rescue our children, Caerulus said in an off-handed tone of voice. *And we'll need your help, Jaiden. Tomorrow you will begin your mission as a spy,*

Oh great, I thought. Why did I ask?

ELEVEN

Search Party

Riding on Skye in the pitch blackness before the hint of dawn lit the eastern heavens, cold air stung my face and kept me awake after a night of tossing and turning. How many times did I rise and stumble over to Baldric, Deryn, and Jarmil's cozy nest expecting to find them sleeping soundly? Each time I hoped the previous day was only a nightmare.

No such luck. The round circle of flat stones, filled in the center with crushed straw, sat cold and empty. Back to bed to relive, over and over, the events from flying high on Skye, to dropping like a rock off Trigger's back, to the mournful shrieks of a devastated mother.

I actually welcomed Caerulus' gruff greeting. *Get up. No time to waste sleeping your life away.*

"Yeah, yeah, Dad, give me a chance to finally get to sleep for a little—"

Up!

He wasn't my father, but he sure did a good impression of him.

Later, Skye and I landed on the mesa where the Council had taken place several days before. I shivered while Hellmuth spouted orders. Then Caerulus, in charge of the search party, barked his own orders. He split Novis and Founders into small groups to spread out across a vast southern open area and search for a band of humans dragging three young dragons to Heaven knows where.

That wide stretch of sand, shallow canyons, and scrub brush between the edge of Septrion and the northern reaches of sparse vegetation seemed beyond our ability to search. And then deeper into the human lands were the forests of the Hills of Alamos, as it's called. My mind reeled, trying to imagine where Hilltop and our humble farm lay. Waiting for a firestorm none of those hill people knew was coming.

Caerulus' voice in my brain made a piercing sound, reminding me of a hawk in pursuit of prey, as he called out names of those he had assigned to each of seven groups. A lot of dragon language, but I could, at least, pick out names, a few of them familiar, most more like gibberish.

Finally getting to the bottom of the barrel, I heard, *Jaiden, go with—*

"Yes, sire! I'll gladly ride Skye since we've worked together for some time now." Not exactly the truth, but I sure worked with her more than any other dragon in this world of ours, including Caerulus and that bandit, Trigger. I added quickly, "And I remembered to bring my trusty slingshot."

What? he said, not expecting anyone, especially me, to say anything in response to his shouting.

Yes, by all means, Skye said in a flat voice, to back me up. *Who else would ride with me? And... he is also skilled with a weapon.*

I sensed a lack of emotion from her, but from Caerulus I felt something like a powerful vibration coming from where he stood on the same rock pile that Hellmuth had stood on during the Council. I think that vibration must have been some kind of strong objection from him directed at his mate and, maybe, me too.

After several uncomfortable moments of silence, he went on but with a lot less energy. *Fine. Next, I want the brothers Lucas and Owyn to go with...*

I lost interest in the proceedings and busied myself adjusting Skye's band that she had me strap on her before we took flight from Azure Den.

"Good. Now I can hang on to you a lot better and not live in fear of falling off. We have flown a lot of miles, haven't we, Skye?" All morning she seemed in a daze, not really mentally with Caerulus and me, so I waited for her response.

Finally, *Yes, Jaiden, we have. I'm sorry I've been so distracted this morning.*

"Hades burn me alive, what else would you be?" I said in a tone a little too bossy. "I mean, you know, with your children taken and all. But we'll get them and I have an idea. I don't know what your mate has in mind, but I think we ought to find the nearest end of a dragon train line. I can't imagine those nasty humans dragging your little ones all the way back to Portville on foot. They'll want to load them on a train quickly so they can get as far away from here as possible."

While the dim light of a dark blue dawn cast its glow on this wild group of restless dragons, my friend Skye leaned down to face me like she had so many times before. The copper flecks in her eyes glowed more like blue shards of glass rather than copper.

You are right. I trust your clear thinking and I appreciate your grief over our loss. I could feel it in the night as you struggled to sleep. I heard your footsteps to my loved ones' bed. I deeply appreciate your concern for us, so let's go now. I don't feel like waiting for Caerulus anymore.

My mind picked up more vibrations of dragon language passing between her and her mate.

With a stronger voice, Skye said, *We are done here. Hang on, we're flying.*

And off the two of us went. The wind of our flight was so gal-durned cold, I nearly passed out, but I held on as the land below slowly took shape and the darkness of night and shadows became silver, then yellow, then the browns and reds of the far-reaching sands.

We rode in silence except for the announcement from Skye that, soon after the two of us left, Caerulus had ordered the search parties aloft to sweep the open area. He cautioned them to stay far enough away from the northern Hills of Alamos to avoid detection by humans.

A little later, in a tone I never heard before from this mighty and confident blue dragon, she said, *I must confess that even before yesterday's awful loss, I... I have had trouble seeing things as clearly as I usually do. I used to see things even an eagle might miss, but not anymore. Things that are small and distant look blurry to me. I don't understand why, but there will be times when I need someone with sharp, young eyes to look ahead.*

"You're kidding, right?" She said nothing. "All right, so you're not playing around with me. I'll do what I can but I really doubt I can see things you can't."

That's all I ask. And we spoke no more about it.

We flew even lower than before with me on her. At times I thought we were going to dive right into the ground.

As the terrain changed from dry sands to hills covered with scattered trees of a more familiar type to me, Skye raised her head and slowed down. She seemed to look over a cluster of hills ahead of us, a little too tall for me to see beyond from my vantage point. Her eyes, still pretty far-sighted, allowed her to detect something ahead.

I see the glint of iron rails. It is the end of the Northern Line into the town of Lynden. I've towed a train or two there over the last several years. Miserable, lonely place.

Not fit for dragon nor man. I do mean, 'man.' Very few women in this town and those that are here... Well, they're not fit to talk about.

I wondered what she meant, but in the next moment, her wings flattened. We dipped down far enough I could almost drag my feet in the dirt. She then reached the tips of her wings heavenward, flapped backwards and touched down, soft as a feather drifting to the ground.

I stepped off carefully trying to get my legs to limber up. The surface was hard and rocky but at least there were a lot of weeds and other greenery that I hadn't seen since first arriving in Septrion.

I felt the tickle of something in the air. I almost sneezed. Yep, we were back near enough to trees, bushes, and grass that made my nose itch and run a little from the irritating pollens.

"Now what? Should we—"

Not 'we.' I am not involved in this next thing. It's up to you. I'll wait here while you climb that big hill ahead. On the other side is Lynden. See if my babies and their captors have made it this far.

She paused. I couldn't even draw a breath. *Then we'll figure out what to do next.*

"Uh, *we* would call for Caerulus, wouldn't *we*?" I croaked.

Perhaps. But we can't know what's next until you go among your fellow humans and find out what's what.

By the Creator of all that lives and exists, this was it. By myself as a spy among my own kind. How was a Hilltop farmer boy supposed to do that?

TWELVE

Ropes and Harnesses

As I made my way down the hill to Lynden, a shiver down my back told me I walked into a trap. It reminded me of when I was among the youngest boys at Hilltop's one-room school. Though everyone sat close together inside the single classroom, the playground outside was clearly divided into age groups with plenty of open ground between. One didn't dare cross that open space without good reason.

When I stepped onto a dusty street at the edge of Lynden, a few people going to and fro looked at me like I was a brat kid invading the big boys' territory. I may have been human like them, but I felt more like a pesky silver dragon among old grouchy blues.

'I don't like this at all,' I thought. I waited for a response.

It will be all right. You're just nervous because you're a stranger here. Though Skye remained out of sight behind a distant hill, she tried to give me confidence with her thoughts in my mind. But an emptiness in my gut told me the opposite.

'I'm coming into town from Septrion. They will know!' my brain insisted. It was weird communicating with Skye through my mind. What if I spoke my thoughts aloud before I could stop myself?

Don't worry about that. Your fear will keep your mouth shut.

'There you go again reading the thoughts I'm trying to keep to myself.' But I looked around and saw narrowed eyes and frowns on the faces of these village people. 'As a kid, I was sent to the big boys' part of the playground because a so-called friend said I could get a really great slingshot from the oldest boy at school.

'But it was a trick and those big guys surrounded me, pulled my pants down to my ankles and left me there for all the girls on the playground to see! I still get teased about it whenever some of those girls pass me by in town.'

I'm sorry that happened to you. Dragon children sometimes do the same stupid things though we don't wear pants, so... I swear I heard a funny sound from her brain that reminded me of a chuckle. Even she's taking a shot at me! I shouldn't have thought anything about that stupid business.

Never mind. You're looking for my children. Quit reliving bad moments in your childhood. Of course, no one has actually seen you before in this town, so act like you belong. No one will stop you unless you do something threatening or if you get too nosy. I can sense their fearful thoughts but all we want to know right now is where my little ones are.

'Be quiet. You're distracting me. I'm now across from the train station. There's the flat-bed car I saw from the hill before I came down into town. A blue dragon is being attached to the front car. Wait a minute. A commotion off to my left. Gol-durn it!

'A bunch of big men with whips have all three of your children tied with ropes and attached to harnesses around their necks and bodies. They're forcing them to climb on the flat-bed. I can see big chain links latched to metal rings bolted to the floor and the men are pulling the youngsters closer to the chain links.'

Oh no! We don't have time to lose. I hoped they had them corralled somewhere before a train arrived to take them away. But the train must have already been waiting before they got here with our children.

'I'm not sure what I can do. Give me a minute to think,' I said back to her. 'Maybe Caerulus and Hellmuth could—'

No time! I'm flying!

"No!" I said out loud. Dang it! A crowd that had gathered to watch the dragons turned toward me with squinting eyes. A few spat on the ground. I forced a smile and uttered a fake laugh like I was amused by what they did to the dragons. I pointed at the dragons and laughed again. Slowly faces turned away from me as the crowd showed their hatred of dragons by hooting and cursing.

The dragon handlers held the young dragons still as others tied the ropes to the chains. I looked back at the hill from where I had descended into Lynden just as Skye shot up nearly to the sun and dipped her head downward. She dove toward the middle of town.

She came in like a bolt shot from a crossbow before the people clustered around the station realized she was there. Skye swooped only an arm's length above the heads of the crowd. She tilted upwards slightly to slap two of the dragon handlers with the tips of her wings before she ascended again. This time, she didn't go very high, but dipped her left wing, rotated and came back toward the train car. All four feet, claws extended, were ready to grasp and slash.

The crowd's reaction, like mine, was delayed by utter surprise at Skye's antics. They finally hunkered down to avoid decapitation by four dragon feet full of claws.

The handlers reacted. In fact, one snapped his whip at Skye, missing her neck only by inches.

"Come closer for a taste of my whip, you blue hellhound!" he roared.

While this aerial display went on, I yelled, "Hang on little ones. It's Jaiden. I'll get you out of here!" That was, maybe, the stupidest thing I could have done, but too late!

I heard Baldric's strong voice in my head. *It's Jaiden, our friend! Mother brought him with her. Come on, let's fight back!*

Yes! Deryn said as she laughed and swung her head at the handler trying to tie her down. The commotion we caused distracted the handler at the right moment. He fell on his face with a groan. Deryn grabbed her ropes with her teeth and tore at them while slinging her head back and forth.

I ran full blast toward the car, jumped on the wooden floor and ripped the ropes away from the handler who had Jarmil, the youngest dragon.

"Jarmil, help me get you loose. Start swinging your head at this creep's face, his hands, anything!"

The handler turned from staring at Skye to look at me with a blank look. "Who is this gol-durned boy? And the big dragon? You idiots, get the Hades out of here!"

Jarmil stunned him with a direct hit to the back of his head.

The handler shielded his head as I jumped up and grabbed the ropes out of his hands. Meanwhile, Jarmil whacked him a second time.

Right then, Skye swooped again, heading for the handlers with her clawed feet. Deryn called out to her older brother, *Down, mother is coming in!*

Both Deryn and Baldric deftly hunkered down to avoid their own mother knocking them off the train. The men weren't quite as skillful at avoidance. Three of them flew off the train car as Skye's feet made hard contact with their faces and shoulders. I had flattened myself on the rough wooden floor, but I quickly jumped back up on my feet ignoring a dozen splinters in my face and body.

I latched on to Deryn's ropes and pulled her and Jarmil off the flat-bed car. "Stay on your feet," I ordered.

Baldric, his anger flaring, drug in his claws, splitting the wood slats under his feet. I clamored to release Jarmil and Deryn's ropes from the chains. Flailing and groaning handlers littered the ground and flat car.

But two handlers recovered from the surprise attack quickly and pounced on Baldric. They wrapped the ends of his ropes around their hands faster than he could jerk and pull himself out of their grip.

Let go, you vermin, Baldric's strong voice shouted in my head, *you piles of dragon manure!*

"That was a good one, Baldric! Now shut up and hang on until I can get the younger ones into your mother's claws."

Skye had turned around over the crowd's heads knocking onlookers around like they were teacups flying off an overturned table. She reached forward with her magnificent wings and pulled herself back toward Deryn and Jarmil on the flat car.

Though the young dragons' harnesses made it easier to control and restrain them, I saw them get in position to give Skye a chance to grab them by those very harnesses. She hovered over the two for a moment, then clasped the central straps that ran down their backs.

She shifted her body and adjusted her grip on each of them probably to be sure she wouldn't drop them. The crowd, stunned into silence in the first several seconds of our attack on the handlers, suddenly found their voices and roared in anger and frustration.

I heard words I never heard before even among some of the rough guys that occasionally came around to help my dad harvest corn and wheat.

I've got them, Skye called out to me as she turned slowly and glided toward us. She gave out a roar as I saw her jaws clamp together fiercely. A small spark flew off her lips. I knew what was coming.

She opened her mouth so wide I could have ridden a horse between her lips without touching teeth. An orange-red flare burst out from behind her long, forked tongue and all hell rained down like a torrent on the train station.

I leaped straight at Baldric and his captors, knocking us off the car onto the hard ground and rails.

"What in Hades is this punk kid doing?" one of the handlers yelled. Since my body was the missile that knocked us down, I landed on top, literally hugging the young blue with the men squashed underneath.

"This is what I'm doing, you, you vermin, you piles of dragon manure," I yelped. Dang it, that was real mature!

More creative curses, groans, and, yes, even screams came out of the mouths of those coarse men. For the first time, I realized I should be scared. Really, deeply, messing-in-my-pants, frightened-out-of-my-head scared. What were they going to do to me for starting this whole thing and toppling a hefty young dragon on top of them as we flew off the flat-bed?

I decided escape was a smart move, so I sprung backwards to get on my feet. I grabbed Baldric's rope attached to the front of his harness, and jerked hard as I could to bring him upright.

I yelled, "Run!" Then turned and pulled him behind me.

Let's go, let's go! Baldric cried out almost as if we were playing a game.

At first, I felt a heavy resistance. But a loss of the tension I felt a moment before quickly followed. I jerked my head back and saw him fighting to squirm his short wings out from under the harness. He couldn't get them out all the way but he pulled them out enough that he caught some air and floated a few feet off the ground.

Look at me, Jaiden, I'm flying! Then his face went from joy to fear. *Kind of flying! But who cares, let's get out here!* he called out, regaining confidence.

This was quite something! Baldric was able to fly at his age because his juvenile wings were long enough that he actually lifted himself above my head. Still, he had to grow more before he could fly the way his parents did. His glide, assisted by my frantic running, helped him rise a little and made my burden lighter.

But it wasn't much of an escape after all. Three boys about my age and unburdened by pulling a gliding dragon, quickly came at us.

"Get the punk, turncoat dragon lover!" one of the boys said. "Don't let him get away like that big blue demon who took the others!"

They tackled me like I was a calf running away from a hot branding iron. Baldric crashed into all four of us piled on the ground under a tree.

Sorry! His voice cried out in my head. *Sorry! I can't get loose!*

His wings tangled in the low branches while the boys quickly rose to their feet. It was easy work to pull him down.

As a knot of mad handlers reached us, I looked up to see Skye circle twice surveying her son and me.

Hang on, she called out.

The handlers grabbed ahold of me with hands stronger than the pliers my dad used to pull out nails. I gave up and was slammed into the ground. They wrapped rope around my wrists and ankles and jerked me back on my feet. I nearly blacked out from the violent treatment but fought to stay conscious.

Ignoring their taunts and rough handling, I looked up.

Skye circled again and, though she said nothing, I sensed her despair as she was pulled between ensuring the safety of the two in her grip and the plight of her oldest and me groveling in the dirt.

She started to descend.

I thought hard. 'No, don't come down here. Go!'

She came down fast, flared fire briefly, then pulled up just beyond the whirling tips of two handlers' whips who recovered enough to try to bring her down. She swooped up and turned her face to me and nodded. I knew what that meant and it was all right.

She dipped a wing to signal good-bye and flew north.

My mind filled with sadness, nearly suffocating me.

Farewell, my brave young man. I have to take the children north, far enough I can land and make sure none of the ropes will cause cuts or choking. But I must leave here quickly because the handlers will organize and chase after us. They know where we live, but if we get close enough to Septrion they won't press on to our cave. Caerulus, Hellmuth and all the dragons will guard not only us but all those in the caves of our land.

There's no going back for any of us dragons, but I can't come back for you now. There's not enough time but I will seek you out when we feel we can make it all the way back to Portville.

Mother, Baldric called out. *Take Deryn and Jarmil. Tell father I will resist and I will not back down.*

I felt I had to say something, too.

'I know,' I thought. 'I understand. You can't bring them right back into danger. Baldric and I will figure this out. These humans don't know we can communicate. They don't know how intelligent dragons are. There are still things we can try and plan without them knowing.

'But don't wait too long. I'm scared and who knows what they'll do to a young male blue dragon and a beat-up dragon lover.'

THIRTEEN

Room and Board

Two guys the size of bulls lifted me off my feet and threw me like a wad of dirty clothes into a dark, frigid cell. I did a face plant into a nasty smelling pile of, I don't know, probably manure... human, maybe. What would be worse, human or dragon manure? Cow manure would be all right because I was used to dealing with it all the time. Whatever it was, there was nothing to clean it off with except for some straw that already smelled like horse pee and felt damp. I didn't really want to know.

"Welcome to your new home," Ubel said. This guy took charge of me after my dragon train ride with Baldric to this massive stone fortress near Portville.

The whole trip I sat blindfolded, hands bound behind my back on a hard floor in a windowless car. When the train stopped, I heard a roaring, crashing sound resembling a big wind coming and going through the tall trees of Emerald Forest. Only when we were in—surprise, surprise—a dark building filled with heavy damp air that smelled worse than any barnyard, could I take stock of my situation.

Terrible. At that moment, I would have given anything to be with my dad on the farm, working my butt off. Instead, I was in a strange place and Baldric was taken away, nowhere to be seen. Before I was dropped into the cell, I spent several hours being questioned relentlessly. Thrown into a filthy cell was a relief.

As I struggled to get on my feet, I heard sounds like crying and whining. I couldn't tell if the sounds came from humans or some kind of animals.

"Anything I can do to help make your stay more comfortable, please let me know," Ubel said. If I didn't know better, I would have thought he said it as if this was one of those rich people's tours. My father talked about such people like Ubel with the same grumble and sneer when he described vandals who steal farm animals and leave the barn burning.

I decided to play along. What did I have to lose? "Thanks so much. This is really quite nice but I'll sure let you know if anything doesn't meet my high standards."

He laughed coarsely. "Anytime, young traitor!" Good. He still didn't know my name but the questioning I had just endured was almost beyond my abilities to hold out much longer.

When Caerulus trained me along with some old wrinkled Founder, Dracul, he made the point that if captured, I couldn't reveal anything about the dragon lands, the fact dragons were there, the kind of dragons, anyone's names, and on and on. Of course, now the humans had found and taken away the three young dragons from Septrion.

Dracul instructed me that I shouldn't even give my own name because they could trace me back to my town and family. That would get ugly with threats to the good people of Hilltop and my dad, such as he was.

The heavy wooden door slammed shut with finality. At least, in this cell, no more "discussion" in that small smelly stone room with no windows and ten blazing torches. They crammed me in there with five of those big bullish guys, each struck me with battle-hardened hands on my shoulders, back, head, arms and legs when my answers weren't suitable. There was a sixth guy, but he stayed in the shadows behind me and didn't make a sound when he slapped the back of my head. Creepy!

Anyway, I answered the brutal questioning with nothing more than to say "no" or "I don't know." The part of the experience that scared me the most were the questions about my town and its people.

"Who are your parents?

"Who trained you to fight the way you did to save those scurvy dragon spawn?"

"Where did you come from?"

And, "Why do you love dragons?"

A slap, a punch, a kick between my legs, a burn from one of the torches, on and on it went, but I said, "No, I don't know!"

My cell did have one big advantage. It was empty, dark, and *quiet*. It stank of urine and poop but I got used to that. I didn't even bother to turn over, but lay there with my face buried in the only dry patch I could find.

"So, who are you?" a shaky voice creaked. I swear it sounded like Old Man Time himself, even older than my great-grandfather before he died when I was six years old.

"Maybe I should know who *you* are," I said.

"Fair enough. The name is Tristram. I've been in here since some big mouth in my little village of Nulltown said I was a dragon lover."

"Oh, you too, huh? That seems to be my new name since I wouldn't give them my real one."

"Can you give it to me?" Tristram's voice creaked.

"Just call me Dragon Lover. But it's not true. I just felt sorry for the dumb little dragons they were wrapping up in those ropes. I can't stand to see animals suffer." That was a pretty good answer. Caerulus would have been proud. I was friendly but provided an answer that meant almost nothing. Only problem was that this old man could be planted there by Ubel.

"Trying to rescue blue dragon young'uns, huh?" His voice seemed to perk up.

"You're pretty sharp for an old man."

"What makes you think I'm old, kid?" he said, rather annoyed.

"Your voice."

"Careful what you assume about appearances and what something sounds like, especially if it's said by Ubel." He coughed and spit. "He and I are also *good friends*. Of course, I don't care for dragons any more than they do, but how can I prove it? No way without a real court of law when it comes to anyone suspected of loving them, much less *helping* those beasts!"

"Yeah, whatever you say," I said and yawned. "Same thing here."

Tristram went quiet. Fine with me. I needed to sleep so I could escape the pain all over my body.

"One more thing before you drop off, young'un. Believe me, I know why you want to sleep after being in the torture room with that lot, but let me take a gander at you."

"You kidding?" I got really tired of this old coot. "Are you so used to the darkness in here that you don't realize there's hardly anything visible? I feel like I'm in the deepest pit of Hades."

"True, but over the years, all the cells have these little bitty holes chipped out of the stone walls so prisoners can see someone else besides the guards and muckers. Go to the back of your cell and work your way forward feeling the wall about chest high."

"If you promise to be quiet after this, I'll do it."

I felt the damp, oily walls. Not sure it was really oil but I didn't want to know. Sure enough, I felt a little hole. I looked through it. I was amazed how a faint light through the bars in the cell door lit up the haggard face of Tristram enough I could see him.

"Oh, so there you are, Tristram. Hello. You look like you need some sleep, too."

"Yeah, the sleep of the grave," he groaned.

"Don't be so glum. Remember we have a friend in Ubel."

"Dragon—you don't mind if I only use your first name, do you? I'm happy to see you are indeed young enough to be my great-great grandson. So, who's your father? Farmer Joe?"

Before I could stop myself, I blurted out, "Farmer? How did you know—?"

"My eyes are better than you think. I can see the tan line around your neck, the sure sign of someone who works outdoors."

"You surprise me, old man. I thought you might be a little slow."

He laughed. "I'm glad we're hitting it off. So, who's your father? Somebody I know? I was a farmer, too, before I went off to volunteer in the Dragon Wars." His laugh became an angry grunt. "Lot of good that did. I get a little huffy about poor treatment of dragons on some of the big farms around my village and I get accused of favoring the dragons after fighting them in the wars."

He coughed violently and spat again. The sound of that was disgusting and I was ready to sleep like the dead.

Unfortunately, he went on, "I think it was someone from my village that accused me, but they got the wrong guy. They could have been talking about that grouchy guy who came down from Hilltop looking for silvers to do farm work. Now *he* was a dragon lover."

I was so tired, that before thinking, I blurted out, "That sounds like my father! He sure didn't care for dragons but he went down to the Nulland Plains and... Never mind."

Tristram regarded me skeptically through that little hole. "I thought as much. Was your father named Gorn?"

I started to deny it but then I realized that *was* my dad's name though I never thought of him as anyone more than 'Father' or 'Dad.'

My silence provided his answer. Dang! This guy was good. Right at that moment, I knew he was put here by Ubel to get the information from me and I fell for it like a stupid fish chomping the worm on a hook! Dad-blame it!

"And..." he continued after a dramatic pause, "your mother was Andena."

If I was silent before, now I was totally mute. No air in my lungs! My mind was in such turmoil, I couldn't think. It was as if one of Ubel's bullies punched me in the chest with both fists.

I barely remembered my father's name, and I only heard my mother's name spoken once. When I was coming out of church years ago, our postman and church pastor, Alden, introduced me to an old lady as Andena's son.

"Bless her heart," the pastor had said.

Although I tried many times to learn more about my mother, my father would clam up and walk away whenever I asked about her. Her family wouldn't tell me anything either, not even how she died. I guess she burned a lot of bridges before she died.

As I kid, I didn't think much about what happened to her. I only knew I missed having a mother especially when I saw how other kids loved and relied on their mothers. Now older, I felt like I was too old to have a mother looking after me. I guess.

At that moment I thought about Skye, and how anxious she was while I tried to rescue her children and how she fought off the train guards. I could only imagine how worried she was about her son, Baldric.

And maybe me?

In any case, it was obvious Tristram was planted by our mutual friend, Ubel. I think I also earned him a big favor by spilling my guts about who I was, where I came from, my dad and our dragon beliefs. Even though Dad didn't really like dragons.

But how did this wrinkled old man in this dark dungeon know who my mother was? The funny thing is, that in spite of wondering how he knew about my mother, I remained silent.

I didn't sleep for a long time. I lay in the smelly straw and waited for some sound that told me Tristram had a visitor or had been taken off to report to Ubel. I heard nothing and I didn't falter for one moment to catch a nap. However, during that time, a dirty little gold dragon was let in through a small trap door to clean up the mess in my cell.

From a bag of moldy bread, he left a clump for my supper on a wooden stool, my only piece of furniture. While half my brain continued to listen for some sound of company next door, I spoke to the gold.

"This is a crappy job," I said, in an effort to seem sympathetic to his situation. But the little gold didn't seem impressed. "I guess it beats doing chores for a grouchy old blue, huh?"

The gold looked at me with vacant eyes. Probably didn't understand human language. I grunted as a way of saying thanks for the bread. His look turned to one of curiosity.

I tried again. "You have a name, little gold dragon?"

He made a whining noise. And then... I heard a little voice in my head, *Dog.*

I was taken aback. "What? Don't you know you're not—No, I guess not."

Not dog. Name, Dog. Hate name. I sensed resentment and I swear the little gold curled his lips and growled softly.

Was this another spy sent in by Ubel? I didn't think gold dragons could communicate at all, so what kind of information would one get out of me, a human? I had to hand it to Ubel, he used every arrow in his quiver!

All this was too much. Capture. Travel to Portville. Taken near the rocky coast along the wide sea. Dropped off at a big, cold stone fortress. Brutal questioning. Thrown in a dungeon. A new fake best friend next door and now Dog, a talking gold dragon!

That's all I needed, a cell mucker in the guise of a stupid but human-hating gold. I realized that Dog or another gold could have waltzed into Tristram cell, picked up a secret written report about me, and waltzed out with the full details for Ubel.

Just too much rolling around in my head! I was exhausted so I fell sleep.

FOURTEEN

Hello… Baldric?

I decided I would play along with Tristram and Dog as
I meekly listened to the old man rattle on about my
new home, the stone fortress. I hoped for some clue
concerning the whereabouts of Baldric.

"When I first came to this hell-hole," Tristram said, "I
came as one of the dragon train soldiers and guards who
get their basic training here. This isn't merely a dungeon

for dragon lovers, it's the Dragon Train Military headquarters for this whole area outside Portville. Mind you, the main battalion of the *regular* Army of the Dear Leader of Humanity is headquartered at the Capitol in the center of Portville. All the cities, towns, villages, and lands throughout the Emerald Forest, the Nulland, the Western Plains and the Foothills at the edge of the barren lands to the north are under the leadership of the Dear Leader.

"And for anything related to the Dragon Train Company, that's where these soldiers and officers in this fortress come in. Ubel is not only the warden but the commander of the dragon train soldiers. By the way, the Big Barn is only a couple of miles west of here."

That got my attention. I'm held captive in a place not far from where I had been two years ago when I helped Skye free her family. So, I wondered if Baldric might have been taken to the Big Barn. I glanced toward the little peeking hole and saw the old man staring at me. I had to say something to change the subject.

"That's rather interesting," I said as I yawned. "As a kid, I remember hearing about the Capitol in Portville and even this *so-called* Dear Leader—"

"Great Creator!" Tristram said as if he were choking. "Don't even suggest disrespect toward the Dear Leader! If anyone of the guards were to hear you..."

"All right. I get it. None of that stuff, even the dragon train didn't mean much to us in little old Hilltop since we were considered the armpit of villages in the forest. The train didn't usually stop in our village."

"It certainly meant something to the men of your village when they went off to war, including your father and your—" His voice choked off, again. "Just... Just keep that kind of attitude and remarks to yourself."

"Sure. You won't hear anything from me. Of course, I was brought here just because I didn't like seeing humans abuse some young dragons. By the Heavens, it wasn't like I was on the dragons' side."

"Anyway, just keep your lips pressed tight. Shut up, in other words."

"Fine."

The old man disappeared from view. I heard him shuffle around and then come back to our little peeking hole. "It seems quiet. I think you got away with your stupid remarks this time. But..."

He didn't need to say more. This was worse than keeping myself clammed up around my father.

Tristram continued his summary of the way things worked in the Capitol. All I was interested in was finding out where Baldric was and how, in all that was holy and evil, I could get us out of this cesspit.

I got bored listening to the old man when two of the big guards came and took me for another love-fest with Ubel.

"Ah, my young friend come in," he said with exaggerated warmth. "Gentlemen, I believe I can trust this fine young man to remain calm while we visit for a while. Please remove the chains, give him a mug of fresh water, and leave us alone."

It stunned me when they did exactly as he said and left us alone. I started to look around the stifling little room in hopes of finding a handy weapon I could use to cave in this creep's head. No such luck.

Ubel commanded, "Eyes front. Don't get too relaxed. I know what you're doing, my friend. Just forget it. I may be friendly but I'm not stupid. I hope we can find a way for both of us to get what we want and each go our own ways. Interested?"

Ubel smiled, raised his hands, palms up and spread his arms almost like he wanted to hug me. It was so ridiculous that I couldn't help but smile. But I did resist making a smart remark. Good thing because I heard something stir behind me. I dared not look back but I now knew we weren't alone in the room.

"I didn't expect such a generous offer but—"

"No, please. Don't turn me down until you hear what I have to say," he said, still smiling.

"Fair enough. Go ahead."

"Thanks," he said in a tone that dripped with false sweetness. "It's simple. We need someone who has been in the northern lands to lead us to where the rebel dragons now live. Now, maybe... we don't know if you were a captive of the dragons or a lover of dragons like a few others of your kind in the uncivilized villages of the Emerald Forest."

That was a little odd since some humans, probably dragon train soldiers, came to Skye and Caerulus' cave and took their young dragons. So, they had a good idea where dragons were. Maybe he was playing games with me or he was too stupid to realize I caught his error.

I resisted a smirk that threatened to twist my lips. I hoped my expression remained as bland as unsalted butter.

Ubel's smile faded and his stare bore a hole between my eyes.

"Sorry," I said, trying to remain bland. "I don't know much about those places."

"That's dragon crap!" he roared. "Plenty of our soldiers who ventured into the miserable dragon lands saw you and your big ugly blue dragon approach Lynden. Your coordinated effort to free that blue cow's spawn was as plain as the smell of your filthy body. Good Heavens! I'm ordering you to get a bath before you return to your cell. I can barely breathe."

Now he was tipping his hand that he knew I was a friend of the dragons. So, what did he really want?

My thoughts were interrupted when I heard someone stir behind me again. The door to the room opened. I heard a mumbled exchange of a few words between whoever was lurking beyond my vision and the guard outside the door. I saw Ubel make eye contact over my head with someone. Ubel nodded.

"Good," Ubel said. "I'm sure you'll also enjoy ridding yourself of your foul body odor. But we're wasting time. I want you to lead a small force of my men into the dragon lands. I want to target all of the dragon caves and not just get lucky with one cave and three young dragons. If not, I'll throw you into a hole in the ground with no light, no clothes, no food, no water, and certainly not another bath!"

"Can I think about it? I get lost easily so I'm not sure I could help you even if I wanted to."

Ubel face turned a dark red and his fists clenched and unclenched nervously. "Dragon crap! Get this scum out of here and forget the bath I just ordered."

"You promised!" I said as a parting shot.

A pair of hands gripped me like steel traps and dragged me back to my cell so quickly, I got dizzy. I was thrown back into the cell just like the first time except I was able to roll left and avoid the smelly pile in the middle of the floor.

The door slammed and locked shut with a riot of rattling wood and groaning metal. A muffled voice yelled, "You have until this time tomorrow to decide about my master Ubel's offer!"

"Thanks, I'll give it serious thought!" No use dropping the friendly little exchanges I had established with Ubel and his minions.

Now what?

As if planned, Dog entered my cell carrying his dirty bag of awful bread. Maybe I could see if he was another of Ubel's minions or if he might be able to help me. I had to somehow make contact with Baldric.

"Dog, can you do something for me?"

No. Don't want trouble. Dog can't.

"Sure, you can. You're a dragon, so do you know Skye, Caerulus, Thanos, Trigger?"

Caerulus. Thanos. Trigger. Yes!

Well, there you are. Either this was good or very terrible news, but before I ended up in a hole in the ground, I was going to give this a shot.

"Listen carefully," I said very quietly to Dog because I didn't want Tristram to hear. I hoped the little dragon would understand very simple instructions. "Go to the Big Barn. Find a young blue dragon named Baldric and tell him this: 'Hi, Baldric. Jaiden lost. Say hi to Jaiden. You all right? Stay here. Don't leave.'"

The little gold looked at me with the most vacant expression in his eyes. I swear there was no brain in that little head. Then, his eyes brightened. *Good. Say Hi. Baldric all right? Dog Jaiden friend.*

"Uh, yeah, I think you have the idea. Come back and tell me what he says."

Dog suddenly got really upset. *No. Trouble. Can't talk. Dragon's trouble. I stay. Not go.*

Of course, what else should I expect from a mostly brainless creature. I tried to reassure him. "No trouble. Dog all right. Just say Hi. Jaiden Hi. Come back."

The gold backed up and ran away as if I was going to jump on him and squash him like a horse fly. "No. No!" I called out to him.

Well, so much for that plan!

I didn't get anything to eat that night, so it was tough going to sleep with a growling stomach even if all I could have expected was moldy bread or wormy pig's feet.

The next morning, Dog tried to sneak into my cell, leave another piece of something that was supposed to be edible and turned to leave very quietly. I sat up with a flurry of hay and dust flying.

The poor little guy let out a squeak like a stuck piglet and scurried to hide behind my poop bucket as if I hadn't already seen him slink into my cell.

"Get out here where I can see you," I ordered. "I saw you come in, but I'm not mad at you, just disappointed."

What disappoint?

"That means I'm unhappy with you. All I wanted to do was to know my young blue dragon friend is all right."

Dog's head shot up. I think he flashed me a smile although it looked like he was baring his teeth at me. *Dog see Baldric. Baldric, Hi. Baldric all right. What now? Baldric says.*

These few words Dog was able to speak were reassuring to me. It sounded like he said Baldric was all right and said, *Hi,* back to me. And he wanted to know what to do now. I realized it was impossible using a dim-witted gold dragon passing his two- or three-word sentences back and forth. I needed to reach out to Baldric and see if he could return messages to me through his mind. Then a crazy thought occurred to me. I wonder if any dragon could send a message that far? It seemed impossible but I had to try *something.*

Skye had spoken in my head from hundreds of yards away. Could Baldric do the same across two miles? That seemed too much to expect especially from one so young. Still... what else could I do?

That night after eating only as much rotten food I needed to keep alive, I asked Tristram, "What direction is the Big Barn from here?"

"No idea. I was blindfolded from the time they hauled me here on a dragon train to when they threw me in this cell after a hard beating."

"Dang! Me, too. All right, never mind."

"Why do you ask? Planning on a little nighttime stroll to the Barn?"

"Not quite." I said no more because I had already said more than I should have because I still didn't trust Tristram.

I sat out of the old man's sight and first faced the door of my cell.

I calmed my nerves and concentrated my thoughts on my memory of the Big Barn and imagined Baldric standing right in front of me. Making sure I didn't speak aloud, I sent a simple message to Baldric.

'Hello, Baldric? This is Jaiden. I sent Dog to see you. Can you hear me?' I hoped that would back up Dog's pathetic little message from me enough that he would trust it was me.

I shifted and faced to my left, then opposite of the cell door, then to my right and focused on repeating the message each time after pausing for a minute or so. I hoped with every inch of my being that Baldric would hear my voice in his mind. I almost lost hope when I heard nothing come back into my empty head. Dang it!

No, I told myself. Don't give up so easily. Try again. I did. Four complete circles. In fact, each time I turned myself a little farther around the circle so if he was located somewhere between the first four directions, I might squarely face him.

Of course, when I thought about it, why would the direction I faced make any difference in how well he might "hear" my thoughts?

Yet on my fourth rotation, I was nearly facing the same positions that I started with when I heard the tiniest little murmur in my head as I faced away from my cell door.

Jaiden? Was that really Baldric's distinct voice sounding a lot like someone I knew from back in Hilltop? The voice was so similar to this young friend of mine who lived just north of my dad's place.

'Baldric? Is that you or am I imagining it?'

Yes, it's me. I sensed his voice more clearly but it was still so faint that a mouse scurrying through the straw on my cell floor threatened to drown him out.

'Baldric! It is you! I know you don't really have a voice I can hear with my ears, but I can tell it's you because in my head you sound different from Deryn and Jarmil! So, you're all right in the Big Barn?'

I'm not all right, but still alive. They watch me a lot and only let me out to eat and poop and pee in the corner of my tiny corral. This brings back bad memories of when I was here with my mother and father. And how sad and scared we were when mother didn't come back.

But then she came back with you and we escaped. Such a happy time. I remember it better than Deryn and Jarmil, so I've told them the story many times. I think they're tired of hearing it.

'Good! You're the chatterbox. So good to hear you. I am in a big stone fortress in a cell. Not nearly as nice as your corral. I have to use a bucket instead of the corner of your corral so it's worse and the food is terrible. Are you eating all right?'

It's food, anyway. More interesting than what we eat in Septrion because here, they feed dragons to have strength to pull trains even though I'm not a train dragon. There are handlers here who remember me and know Caerulus and Skye are my parents. I don't like the way they look at me and talk about me in low voices. I'm scared they will hurt me or use me to hurt my mother and father.

'Don't worry about that right now. I'm going to escape from here, but I don't know how. Cooperate with the handlers. Don't let them think you're looking for trouble. You might even act like you're not at all like your parents. Be friendly with the handlers, do whatever they say. But... if they take you out and you feel scared, try to escape. You're big enough you could really hurt them if you have a good chance.

'If you're scared, that means you can feel their bad thoughts. Not like you can know my thoughts, but blue dragons can understand human thoughts and you know people's language almost as well as your parents.

'I hope they don't try to hurt you before I can get to you, but be careful and don't make trouble. At least, not yet, anyway. Understand?'

Yes. My mother had a talk with me not too long ago about such a thing. I think she had a bad feeling something like this might happen when the humans started to come into our land. Dragons want to be left alone, but people won't allow that for long.

'You and your parents are right. The time is not now, but I hope soon. I will talk with you every night until I can figure something out.'

I knew that was not only wishful thinking, it was, as my dad would say, "Stupid! How stupid can you be?" But I couldn't dash the young dragon's hope because if he got a chance to escape without me, that would be great. Then I wouldn't feel so sorry for myself if Baldric got away. Somehow, in all this crap that was happening, I realized it wasn't just about me and it wasn't just about my fear of missing out.

It was about saving the lives of these amazing beings, the blue dragons and especially those that made up Skye's family. I finally admitted to myself that Skye was the most important, uh, being in my life. Though I guess she wasn't a person, she was more than a person...

I tried not to think about it too much. I was afraid of what could happen next so I stuffed dark thoughts deep within me and just hoped I could do something or think of something to get Baldric out of this mess.

Jaiden? Are you still there?

'Oh, I'm still here, all right. Not going anywhere for a while. But, like I said, I will talk to you every night. I don't have any plans yet, but be careful and watch out for anything suspicious.'

I will.

'Good. I'm tired of thinking and talking to you this way and trying to hear everything you're sending to me. Let's rest. Good night, sleep tight.' I'm not sure he understood that silly old human saying. The only times I would hear that were the times when I stayed with my grandmother, my mother's mother. She was a kind old lady and would take me off my father's hands when there wasn't much work on the farm.

I guess she felt my father and I needed a break from each other. I still missed her. I sure didn't want to miss Skye like I missed my grandmother.

I finally took a deep breath to loosen up my tight chest and stiff neck.

"You still awake?" Tristram asked in a shaky voice.

"Barely. I think I'm as tired as you sound. Good night."

"Good night. I got a little worried because it was so quiet in your cell," he said, almost apologizing.

I really wanted to trust him, but I still couldn't.

"Good night old man."

"Sleep tight, youngster," he said with a chuckle.

Now that was creepy. He almost quoted exactly what I said to Baldric.

It was pleasantly quiet until I heard a noise in the cell on the opposite side away from Tristram's. Weird. That was an empty cell.

Except now it wasn't.

FIFTEEN

New Neighbor

The nice, deep tiredness that had always allowed me to fall asleep almost instantly, failed me once I heard the noise in the other cell. I wondered who Ubel threw in there but I didn't feel like asking or getting acquainted. As it turned out, I should have tried because it was a good two hours before I finally drifted off to a restless sleep. For all my worry and wondering, I never heard another sound from that cell.

That is until the next morning. "Hey, who's in there? Does your cell stink as bad as mine?" The voice was bright and had real authority. Maybe it wasn't a prisoner, but one of the tough guards that Ubel put in charge of Tristram and me. Only one thing, it was a woman's voice!

"What?" I said, pretending like I hadn't understood what was clearly said. "Who are you? This is a prison, not a playground."

"Oh, really? I heard you came from some rathole town where it stinks as bad as here and it's more like a prison."

I stood up and stomped over to the little hole on the wall opposite the one that opened on Tristram's cell. "Bring yourself over here so I can see—"

"Like this, sleepy head? You snore like an old sow pig, but now I see a little bit of your face that you're just a boy."

"I'm not a boy! I'm a guy just like you're, uh, well, like you're a grown up woman."

What I saw through the little hole was hard to describe because of the dim light. Since it was early morning, only the slightest bit of gray light leaked into the cells. But I could see parts of the face of a woman. Hard to tell how old she was, but she sounded older than me and I only saw her eye, a little bit of nose, and a shock of blond hair draped over her eye like a loose blanket.

Her strong voice came through the hole as if her mouth was next to my ear.

"All right, sorry, I'm not insulting you," she said. "Ubel told me he had a boy in the cell next to mine. I can clearly see you're about my age, though I can't tell if you're big or little, fat or skinny. You sound like my young brother trying to be tough." She laughed.

I wasn't offended by her laugh because when she tilted her head back, I saw her mouth revealing lovely full lips, straight teeth, and a strong chin. As she moved around, I saw what looked like a slender face, and skin that seemed, even in the dim light, to be smooth and firm. If the rest of her matched what I could tell about parts of her face, wow! My imagination went crazy. She *could* be the most beautiful woman I had ever seen.

"I'm not trying to be anything," I finally said. "I didn't expect a woman in these cells. Not at all. I'm accused of loving dragons and they must think I'm dangerous, otherwise why would they lock me up like this. But you? What could you have said?"

"I didn't say anything. I'm not one to waste time with words, though right now, I don't have much else to do but spin words for a boy—sorry," she laughed. "A young guy."

I heard her stride around her cell. She spoke, but I had to strain to hear her clearly. "I made it plain in my town that those poor beasts are getting a rotten deal from our stupid leaders and those crooks who run the dragon trains. I thought I was among friends when I spoke my mind. Friends who felt the same as I, but I was wrong. Someone betrayed me and so, here I am."

Yeah, there she was with a guy in the next cell who doesn't want to miss out on a crazy adventure while behind me was some old man who was likely a spy planted by Ubel to get the goods on me. And, of course, there was this dumb gold dragon who may or may not care one thing about me, but, so far, might be useful.

Tristram interrupted the questions swirling in my head, "Hey, who's the woman? What's a woman doing in this forsaken crap hole?"

"Well, Tristram, this is... I don't know. Who are you?" I asked the woman.

"Call me Wyetta. The daughter of outcasts in the village of Cedar Grove. Our town's a little collection of cattle ranchers stuck between the Nulland Plains and the South Emerald Forest."

"I've heard of that town," I said. "You're about half way along the train tracks between my town of Hilltop and Portville. Did they come and get you in Cedar Grove?"

"No, I was with a band of like-minded young people, mostly ranchers in the area. We were heading into the forest to link up with some others who my comrades said lived in the villages in the hills. We walked right into an ambush. Someone among us set us up! And when I find out who..."

The way she spoke made shivers run down my spine. Something in her voice, a kind of toughness and determination that I never heard in a man, much less a woman, made me nervous. Who was this Wyetta, anyway?

"Shut up in there, this isn't a social hall!" a guard yelled.

"You shut up, Ubel minion!" Wyetta shouted back.

"I think we better be quiet and just eat our breakfast," the old man cautioned in a low voice.

"What? I can't hear you," Wyetta said.

"Come on, please," I said even more quietly than Tristram had spoken. "Don't get us all in trouble. It's been bad enough."

She sighed so deeply I think it was more a performance than a natural reaction. "All right. I don't want to make trouble for you two. As for me, I don't care."

Several minutes of silence dragged by. I braced for one or two of the biggest guards to bust in and kick my butt. Nothing happened.

Finally, Dog wandered in with his usual smelly bag of left-overs. Too bad I couldn't fit through that tiny trap door of his. I took my portion and sat in the growing grayness. I almost wished I could eat in darkness so I couldn't see things crawl around in my food. But the quiet was good.

With luck Wyetta might stay quiet so we wouldn't get beaten for disturbing the peace. We did get our meal, so there was that, though this terrible excuse for food was punishment enough!

Later that day, I whispered through the hole to Wyetta's cell. "Thanks for staying quiet. I thought we were in for it after all your shouting."

"Sorry, I got worked up. It's only been two days since we were captured. I think some of the guys with me were killed. I haven't seen any of them since. We resisted as much as we could but there were too many of those dragon train thugs who took us prisoner. We shouldn't have tried to gather so many people who wanted to stop the terrible way dragons were treated. We tried too hard and people figured out what we were really doing.

"We had gotten off a train near my village and headed out across open land. We came to a bunch of cedars—ironic, huh? Me, being from Cedar Grove. Those thugs nailed us before we could fight back.

"I'm just so mad at myself!" she said quietly, though there something almost like a deep rumble in her chest. I don't think I had ever met man nor woman who had so much emotion bottled inside. Except for my grouchy father

I felt like I had to tell her how I ended up in this hellhole. "Yeah, well, I got in with a couple of dragons who were captives of the dragon trains. I, uh..." I realized that though I naturally trusted this woman more than I did Tristram or Dog, a sharp stab of doubt rammed through my stomach. I suddenly felt I should not say too much, even to Wyetta.

"I worked with some dragons, too," she said wistfully. "They're better than people. Not too bright, though. Those that can spew fire are strong and dangerous as all Hades. But they fight smart. And it's obvious they'll do anything to escape captivity. I guess somehow, they just want to be left alone and be free."

"Yeah," I said, not sure what else I should say. "I kind of got that feeling myself, but all I did was defend some young dragons from being abused and taken away from their parents."

"That's kind of cute, calling them 'parents,'" she said. "Never thought of them that way, but I guess that's what they are if they hatch little dragons. In a way, they are just like cattle who breed and have calves except they come out in big eggs before they hatch. But you gotta admit that only people *raise* children. You know, teach them right from wrong, how to take care of themselves, and the things we believe in like Heaven and Hades, you know, Hell. All that stuff."

Maybe I ended up saying too much even when I was trying to use my worn-out excuse that I was just trying to save the dragon children from mistreatment. Still, she was really sincere even if a little ignorant about how smart dragons were. I think it was at that moment, I began to trust her even more.

The days that followed those first conversations with Wyetta found me sharing more and more with her as she explained how she and her friends had already done some undercover work to help the dragons. It seemed Skye and Caerulus were not the only dragons that didn't want to tow trains. Wyetta said she and her friends helped all kinds of blue and silver dragons, like those who worked on farms and ranches and along the coast where a lot of heavy work was forced on bigger dragons. She didn't think much about the golds, though. More like pests. I had to agree on that one, though Dog had been a little helpful.

But all good things come to an end, too. One day, I was dragged out of my cell even before I finished my breakfast of chicken soup that tasted like it had sat out for a month.

"I can't say I missed you much," I said to Ubel, trying to be funny as I was dumped in his miserable little room.

Once the door closed, a third unseen guard slapped the back of my head.

"No, no, not so hard!" Ubel frowned and admonished the unseen guard in mock concern. "This one has been very friendly to me. I just know he is ready to help our cause to finally squash this foolish dragon business. Aren't you, Jaiden?"

"Of course, anytime. Just say the word and I'm your servant," I replied, mocking him in equal measure.

"Good. Now let's get down to business without further games. All right?"

"All right." That was it. I decided to play this game to the hilt and see how far I could stretch it. Maybe do something that would make a real difference and save the day for Baldric, who I hope was still in the Big Barn. And possibly help myself and Wyetta.

I believe at that moment, I was determined to show her I could be a hero, too, and put myself right in the middle of big things. No more fear of missing out!

Now if I just had some idea of what to do next. There were too many unknowns including my cellmates on both sides of me and that goofy Dog. Assuming I had even a shadow of what to do and I started talking in my sleep, it could bring about both Baldric and my deaths or at least a lot of misery. So in case something came to me, I had to keep it hidden deep in my brain.

I realized Ubel was staring at me. Could he read my mind right then?

"So, Jaiden, here's the deal," he said. "I can release you if you're willing to lead us to where the older dragons from the Dragon Wars have lived north of Lynden for years. We know you were somewhere along the edges of the area they occupy, but we want to strike precisely at the center of where those troublemakers live. Especially the old timers from the last days of the Dragon Wars. We can't waste time and blood wandering around looking for dragon caves.

"I told you, I don't know—"

"Quit lying, Jaiden!" Ubel blared. "You were seen by some of my dragon train men in Lynden arriving from the north. I told you I don't care about those who have escaped from the trains, farms and such places like those who spawned the three dragon cubs or whatever they're called. Those dragons have no battle experience and they can't spit fire. But the old ones... Do I have to spell it out for you?"

"No. I wasn't anywhere near any dragons. But... I feel sorry for them, and that's all. I didn't like the way they were treated by your people in Lynden."

"Would you like to die along with your worthless friends in the prison cells?"

"Of course not!" I said with as much force as I could manage.

"We don't understand how the old ones operate," he continued, "but they're something like a real smart wolf pack who can strike and retreat while luring humans into an ambush. It almost worked for them many years ago, but we learned a thing or two and drove the survivors far away into the miserable deserts of the north. It was all before your time, but now you can help us end the existence of dragons forever."

Either he was testing me or maybe he didn't really know what I was thinking. I could only go ahead with this and hope he was blind to my real thoughts and feelings.

"Why should I help you destroy all the dragons?" I said. "If they wanted to put themselves under human rule, they would have done that long ago like cows, horses, goats, and all the rest of farm animals. But they're, uh, well, they're wild beasts wanting to be free like wolves, elk, even small animals like squirrels, birds and such." I wasn't sure if I was pushing too hard. I had to seem more willing to be "reasonable" and make a deal because the frown on Ubel's face wasn't encouraging.

I had to say something else or he would quickly change the subject. "All right, that's neither here nor there," I blurted out. "I just tried to make sure people were treating those young dragons right. Like they might treat calves or ponies. It was hard to watch. But you've made a good point and I'm willing to help if you agree to something first."

"What?" the big man growled. I think he was quickly losing patience playing games with me.

"That young woman you brought in recently," I said "She is a lot like me. She's a rancher and she no more approves of animal cruelty than I do, but she has been around more dragons than I have. A lot more." At this point, I knew I had to admit I had been among the dragons because they knew I came into Lynden from the north with Skye when Baldric, Deryn, and Jarmil were captured. This was going to be tricky.

"Well, maybe I've been around dragons a little more than I first said," I mumbled, acting like I was reluctant to admit the truth. "A dragon captured me in my hometown, Hilltop. I didn't have much choice, but the big old thing scared me half to death. I had to go along with it when she—it escaped from towing a train. I didn't know a thing about how to fight or escape from a dragon. She could have stomped me into the ground, and she was so big—"

"I knew it!" Ubel said as he slapped the top of the small table in front of him. "I knew you had to be that stupid kid who slipped the big female blue away from the dragon train in Hilltop. You little creep! You gave our men a lot of grief."

I heard a sharp gasp behind me, but I forged ahead, pretending I didn't hear it.

"I know, but I was so scared. You may think dragons are stupid, but she knew to keep me close and not give me a chance to escape. I don't know why she let me live after that, but I showed her I can hunt when I got hungry. And if I hunted for myself, I had to share what I caught with her, otherwise... I would have been her meal! They're dangerous because dragons are so big, they fly, and they can kill a kid like me in nothing flat!"

He seemed satisfied with what I said as he smiled slightly at me and leaned back in his chair. "So, you know something about the northern lands where the dragons are?"

"Not much. Finally, that big blue dragon dragged me up north just beyond Lynden where we joined some other escaped dragons. I haven't seen the big old blue dragons from the wars up close, but I have a good idea where they are because whenever they flew overhead, I saw where they headed from time to time."

"So why should I take along this troublesome female I just locked up?" He was baiting me. Either I was going to blow it all or I had to say the right thing to get him to consider my plea.

"Like I said, she's been around them more than I. She said as much to me. I didn't have much of a clue until I heard her talk about them..." Now here came the risky part. I had to do this right or I would squander the most important thing about the dragons the humans still didn't know.

I continued. "They're smart in a, I don't know, a kind of wily way, like you said, like smart wolves. But not at all smart like humans. She knows that. The north lands are huge and it's easy to get lost out there. And since dragons fly... well I don't need to spell it out for you. I can take you right to that small bunch of younger dragons by a safe route. Then once you eliminate them, I can take you to the area where I think the old blue dragons are. That female in the cell next to me knows a lot about how dragons act and respond to danger. How they can track humans, stuff like that. We'll all be safer with her along. And I know where they are. You need both of us."

There I had said it. Was it enough? Was it too much? Does he even need me or her now? Would he chop off both our heads and move towards Septrion on his own? I know he can find Novis where my dragon friends are, but would he want to get at the old, battle-tested dragons so badly that he will take us along? I hope he did and that he thinks only I can lead him to the Founders, otherwise, he'll kill us right now.

His smile had faded as his mouth became a wide flat line. I feared whatever he did, he probably had his own reasons no matter how weak my reasons were for taking my cell neighbors along. Like maybe he wanted a good excuse to kill us all after he found the dragons.

Ubel's eyes glazed over as if he was in deep thought. Then his chin loosened a bit and his mouth opened. What had he decided?

I couldn't breathe and my heart stopped.

SIXTEEN

Three Dragon Trains North

"You have a deal," Ubel told me. I nearly collapsed, face down on the floor, but somehow, I managed to stay in my chair. "But if I get a whiff of betrayal, I will let loose my men on you and... the woman. She'll get it worse than you do, but you won't be alive to see it. Maybe. Maybe I *will* let you live long enough to see her get her just rewards if this is a trick, dragon lover!"

"I'm not a dragon lover," I said as humbly as I could manage. "But I'll have to prove that to you, first. So, let's get going."

Ubel smiled and slapped the top of his table again, but he was laughing this time. "Great! I'll order real food tonight for the lot of you."

"That's very welcome, but one more thing. Actually, two things. I want Dog, the little gold dragon and old Tristram to come along. They also know a thing or two about the dragons that I don't and—"

"Forget it! The old man is useless and will only slow us down. And that gold is too stupid to be of any use. I have two silvers and their gold riders who are young and ruthless that will accompany us along with a battalion of fifty men. This isn't a walk in the meadow. This will be an invasion with a small enough force we won't be seen until it's too late. Yet we'll pack enough punch to scatter those old blue heaps of dragon crap like rats trying to escape a fire!"

I started to protest, but maybe he had a point. The old man and the little gold wouldn't be much use, but I hated to leave them behind because no matter what happened, their deaths would be ordered as soon as word about whatever was going to happen in Septrion got out. If the dragons won, they would be pitiful objects of scorn to be tortured and killed. If we lost, they would be suspected of betrayal in the humans' last-ditch effort to eliminate friends of the dragons.

That truth hit me hard. My request for their companionship was a to-be-fulfilled death sentence for them just because I selfishly wanted them to come along on the chance of saving them. Even not knowing what might really happen to them. As my stupid move fully dawned on me, I saw Ubel's face slowly break out in a sly smile like that of a fox who's cornered a helpless rat.

"Sure, Jaiden, whatever you say. Sorry, I jumped to conclusions. Of course they can come along for the party," he said all too smoothly.

Dang! Dang it all to Hades and back. My stupid effort to bring them along meant I had betrayed them and myself to a sure death. I couldn't even guess if they would be killed right then or later after our mission headed north or upon news of whatever would happen in the next several days.

I had it all wrong. We were ready to leave for Septrion the next day and Ubel, in a magnificent performance of generosity, actually allowed Tristram and Dog to come along with Wyetta and me. Near the head of the entourage, we were placed in an open-roof train car near the blue dragon that towed the first of three trains headed north for Lynden.

Ubel probably wanted all four of us scum prisoners within reach of his sword if anything went wrong. Whatever the reason, I knew it wouldn't be good. Oh, well!

The sides of the train car were high enough it would be impossible to climb up and over to escape. A small canopy protected us from the sun while we sat on cushioned seats.

Dog had a bed of straw to lay on and a barrel of fresh water and a big trunk of tasty, dried food was available whenever we wanted to eat. If this was our last journey in this life, at least it would be a pleasant journey to death.

The night before, we all were taken to a larger room in the fortress and treated to decent food and drink. I'm sure the roast chicken the prison workers served couldn't stand up to those raised on my dad's farm, but at that moment it was like the food served in Heaven! We even had a glass of wine that tasted like sunshine instead of mere water to accompany a fine, but simple meal. Anything at that point was better than the rotten, moldy cast-offs we usually ate.

Tristram stood with some difficulty and offered a toast. "If this be our last meal, let it rest gently on our stomachs while we go out in style."

"Oh, come on, old man. Have some confidence this might end well," I said less than half sure I was speaking the truth.

"It's all right, Jaiden," Wyetta said. "This is not a time to fool ourselves. I don't know how you did this, but—" she stopped and looked around. Our usual guards were stationed just outside the doors of this most comfortable room. "You have to agree, it is beyond anyone's wildest imagination. Although this may not mean better days ahead, let's not be foolish. Instead, let's simply enjoy every day to come as if it were our last. No one knows what will come next in these uncertain times. Here's to humanity and the downfall of the dragons," she said as she winked at me.

"Hear, hear!" both Tristram and I shouted. Dog even made a little cackling sound as if in agreement.

As I drank the toast, I had my first good chance to look over Wyetta and see the whole woman instead of bits of her face through the little hole in our cells. She was tall and slender though I could tell she was very fit, probably from working on a ranch. I was a little surprised by her clothing. She wore the typical rancher's sturdy shirt and pants but the material of those clothes was a lot finer than my old raggedy brown cotton tunic and heavy farmer's trousers. They were brown like mine but the fabric was made of special material, something like linen instead the heavier cotton of my work clothes.

She looked better in those rancher clothes than most girls in my village of Hilltop did when they dressed up for church. I carried the image of her back to my cell, laughing and talking with the rest of us like she didn't have a care in the world.

Well, that remained to be seen—for all of us!

The next day, we boarded our train car as scores of soldiers filed into covered cars of our lead train and the two trains behind us. My stomach nearly leaped out of my mouth when I saw two silvers and their gold riders stride out of a small barn connected to the fortress and enter one of the train cars just behind us like they owned the place. To see golds riding silvers again after the horrible battle Skye and Caerulus fought during our escape from the Big Barn two years before chilled me down to my toes.

The reality of the situation sat heavy on my heart. What have I done? Not only did I insure my new friends would die soon, but will this end the dragons' dream to be free? Or it could finally lead humanity to realize that they aren't the only ones who deserved to live free. I feared many on all sides will die.

But the big question that started to nag me was would any of us be left or would the whole world gain peace, free of people and dragons with only the simpler creatures who survive?

Those thoughts oppressed me while we rode along. To help ease the burden I had placed not only on myself but on all humanity and dragons, again, I thought back to the previous night after the celebration dinner. Back in our cells, but with comfortable beds brought in and a pleasant little candle to burn all night to keep us company, I decided I had to reach out to Baldric before I was taken beyond any possibility of sharing our thoughts.

I faced in the same direction as before when I could finally hear the quiet thoughts of the young dragon.

'Baldric? Are you there? I have news!'

There was a long pause. Was I too late? Did Ubel order his death or banishment to some dreary farm far out on the Nulland Plains?

I am here. It is good to hear your thoughts again, Jaiden! I was almost asleep. Your thoughts are strong tonight. What's happened?

'I'm either on my way to gain the freedom of dragons and the destruction of a powerful human leader or...' I tried to gather my scattered thoughts so I wouldn't scare him with my deepening fears. 'Or I'm taking myself and new friends here at the fortress down the road to disaster and probably put your life along with all your family and the rest of the dragons in Septrion in serious danger!'

A long silence.

'Sorry. I don't mean to scare you,' I continued, 'but if there's no way to escape soon, then see if you can get yourself taken off to a farm somewhere before the worst happens.'

What in the name of our Great Dragon Spirit do you mean?

'I have made a deal with the warden of this fortress prison. I am going to lead him to the part of Septrion where your parents and their fellow Novis live. My hope is to lead a human army into a place where they might not win a fight. This could lead to something big. Either something terrible or something good for all dragons. I just don't know, right now.'

Why?

I could sense the fear and sense of betrayal in his thoughts, as if he had screeched them out loud.

'My time left in this world could be coming to an end. I can't see a way to escape this horrible place. Those I've met here are powerless as well. But maybe I can do something—I don't know. But I promised to lead Ubel, that's the warden here, to the very place of the Novis, those new to the dragon lands like your mother and father. I told him I had an idea of where the Founders are, too.'

Still, I ask why?

'I told you, I could tell he was past ready to kill me and the others in the cells next to me. I don't know anything about others held prisoner in the fortress, though I hear cries and wailing most all the time. I felt like I would either die soon for nothing or I could try to lead these humans to disaster.'

But that won't be the end of it. You know that!

'I don't know anything for sure. I'm pretty sure you don't either, as young as you are. But, one thing for sure, it will give the humans something to think about.'

Yes, it will. It will reveal where the dragons live in the northern desert and it will make the humans even madder.

'Well, there's that. But I don't want to simply get killed and miss out on what happens next. Especially if there's a chance for dragons, to, to be free. Maybe they can win this fight.'

He was very quiet for a long time. I figured he shut me out of his mind because he was mad. And maybe so he could savor the memory of his parents and his brother and sister before they were taken from this life.

I lay down and wondered if I would sleep enough to get me through the journey to come. I tried to quiet my thoughts.

As I drifted into a deep blackness, words came to me so gently, that at first I thought I only imagined them.

Good luck. Be careful. That is all. Bye.

That was Baldric but I could barely put a thought together to send back to him. I had to say something that offered a little hope.

'Bye. I know I'll see you soon.'

As our odd foursome prepared to board the dragon train, Ubel pulled me aside. My only thought was, "Oh, good. Now he's going to throw me back in my cell and take my new friends on this adventure without me!"

Instead, he grabbed the neck of my tunic and pulled my face into his and smiled like a hungry wolf before devouring a bleating sheep. "Don't get me wrong. You haven't fooled me one bit. If you try anything funny, you and your buddies will be fed to the dragons pulling these trains. You're taking us to the dragons in the northern desert, not an empty canyon. No stops for you four. You get on the train and you stay on the train until we head out cross country to the dragons' caves."

Ubel paused a moment. "If I even smell the whiff of betrayal or a stupid joke, you're dead!" He smiled again and, I swear, I saw blood drip from the corners of his mouth.

"Yes, sir. You'll see," I said in a squeaky voice that would have embarrassed a suckling piglet.

The trip north took a lot longer than I expected because when I was taken south from Lynden after my failed effort to save Baldric, it was no more than two days later until I was thrown into my lovely cell. I guess all the soldiers and equipment added a lot of extra weight.

The joy of travel and freedom wore thin as we were jostled around by the train climbing high up into the Emerald Forest, dipping down, then up uncounted valleys, even passing through Hilltop. I didn't think I would know when we passed through my town, but I heard a familiar sound. The call of our neighbor's old cow who was always anxious to have a bull visit her for a few days. Her invitation echoed down the hills into the village just as the train slowed as we passed through.

I couldn't see over the train car walls to catch sight of something familiar, but that sound and the smell of the village bakery were unmistakable.

"Hey, Dad," I whispered to myself, "sorry I can't drop by and help milk the cows. Say a prayer for me and my companions. No telling how this will go..."

"What was that?" Tristram asked.

"Oh, nothing. Just mumbling an old prayer I learned as a kid."

"Seems like a good idea, mention me too. I don't know how much longer I can take this trip. My old bones are wearing thin with all this bumping and swaying."

"Don't complain, ancient one," Wyetta said with a smirk. "It's not much fun for us younger ones, either."

I turned and gave her a good long look without embarrassment since her attention was on Tristram. Dang, she was a fine-looking woman. Tall, lanky but with the defined muscles of one who worked outdoors. When I first saw her entire face and body a few days earlier at our little celebration dinner at the fortress, I realized how stunning she was. I felt small and lackluster next to her. Still, she treated me like a good ol' friend instead of a clueless idiot, so there was that.

Tristram, of course, actually looked better in good light. His wrinkles were all there and his scrawny body was about what I expected. But there was a toughness, like an old leather jacket that may have been ugly but still offered protection from the harshness of hard work and the chill of a winter wind.

I imagined I looked rather pathetic in comparison. Dirty clothes in disarray, face burned from sun and wind, thin body deprived of solid country food for far too long. Oh well, all this wouldn't matter when we arrived in the midst of the Novis.

With no more than a shaky hope and confused ideas to save our necks swimming through my mind, I looked above watching the sky start to turn dark yellow as if the day lasted too long. Soon we would be in Lynden and what was going to happen then?

SEVENTEEN

Trek to Septrion

Our arrival in Lynden stirred up a lot of noise. Except instead of a near riot of humans screaming for Baldric's and my head like before, they celebrated. A small band of musicians played lively tunes while drunken citizens sang songs about frying dragons with their own flames. Lovely things like that.

At least they treated our little foursome almost like heroes instead of traitors. What if everything went wrong? For now in this town, we pretended to hate dragons and so we were celebrated. But they celebrated Ubel and his battalion of hardened soldiers even more. They had quite the party on into the night while we cooled our heels in a comfortable train car under constant armed guard, of course. Still, the food was good and the racket of celebration was far enough away, I looked forward to a good night's sleep after the last few tough nights on a moving train car.

Thinking back over the past few days while we had traveled along, I had noticed the train dragons changed twice every day so that a fresh dragon pulled us each time. If the weight of the men and their armaments had not been so heavy, it would have been a quicker, smoother ride. Now with the train ride over, I calmed my mind for a restful sleep by thinking back to the long steady climb four miles past Hilltop as we reached the highest point of the entire journey.

I had wandered to the front of our car dragging my chair with me. I stood on the chair and looked over the high walls of the car. I watched for that brief glimpse when, on a clear bright day, I could see the brown and tan horizon of the desert far to the north. I stepped down and sat. For me that was unusual because I had not stayed still long enough to sit for very long since we left the fortress in Portville.

I entered a quiet place in my head, closing out the world around me. For the first time in days, my mood was good while I sat apart from my companions in our open air car. I'm sure I looked like some weird religious fanatic sitting and meditating on what only the Creator knew. But that was all right because they didn't talk to me or bother me while I concentrated.

Soon, the train descended into the next deep valley. At that point, the desert where the dragons lived would not come back into view until we arrived in Lynden. My good mood faded so I got up and walked toward my companions smiling sheepishly when a sensation like a fierce wind blew through my body.

Hearing that familiar voice in my mind filled me so much I had to fight the urge to yell "hooray" and simply keep my expression bland while I turned around and returned to sit at the front of the train car like nothing happened.

I needed a mental housecleaning and though it wasn't fun to go over the mistakes I had made in the days following capture in Lynden, it had to be done if I wanted to keep my sanity and a tiny piece of self-respect. My mood swung from relief to fear to joy to regret, but I had to clean out the cobwebs in my mind until we reached Lynden in the next day or two.

I still regretted leaving Baldric behind but I hoped the Big Barn would be safer than this journey. It had to be.

Still, recent events had turned out worse than the times in my youth when I had gotten myself into stupid trouble. I was good at being an idiot at school showing off for my friends and trying to impress the bigger kids by antagonizing the teacher. Of course, I caught the worst kind of hell, first from the teacher and then my dad when I got home. And I knew he knew about my breeches of conduct before I darkened our door. No need to explain anything to him. How did adults do that? Some kind of mind-talking like the dragons?

Aware again of riding on the dragon train, dread filled my heart because lives were at stake. Not just my life which I hardly cared about. But the lives of my new friends, poor brave Baldric stuck back in Portville, Skye, Caerulus and their family, plus all the dragons up north. What would happen to them? Would everyone die?

Probably. But only if I failed.

However, after arriving in Lynden, I drifted off and slept well. Maybe because I had no energy left. What came next could certainly tax every ounce of energy I could muster. So I slept.

The next morning, after the celebration, we were taken off the train. Just outside the car where we spent the night, our guards patted us all over and checked for anything we carried in the sacks we threw over our shoulders. Anything resembling a weapon would have spelled a quick end to our personal journey. A third guard approached. Something familiar about the way he walked took my breath away.

He pulled off his leather helmet and spoke, "So, the farmer boy still thinks he's a big shot, huh?"

Oh, my Creator, Clod! What's with this guy? Some kind of demon that could fall off a train and explode in a cloud of dirt and blood and then resurrect himself like a supernatural being? He came right up in my face and looked down on me, as if I were a field mouse. He hit my chest with a fist like iron.

"After you and the big blue stole that dragon train, you thought you killed me when I fell off, didn't you? Well, I broke a few bones, but here I am all mended and ready to kick your butt up through your neck if anything goes wrong on our little trek to the north."

At that point, I lost all concern for my health. "Where did you come from? I didn't see you."

"Well, I've been watching you, punk! Remember all those times in the fortress when some unseen person breathed down your neck or slapped you up the side of your empty head?"

What? "Well, yeah, but—"

"That was me, loser! I told Ubel the story of how you and I first met, so he thought it would be hilarious if I did a few fun things behind your back like some kind of demon ghost punishing you for your sins and stupidity. Worked, didn't it?"

He laughed and coughed up slimy phlegm from the back of this throat. He spit at my face, but I dodged fast enough to only get some of it on my neck. "Just a little condition I have now after my fall off the train. You need to have every speck of my spit thrown in your face for that. I don't believe this turnabout in your feelings about dragons. I won't go against my boss, but my time to kick your butt up between your ears will come later."

With that, he tromped away to join a small platoon of soldiers, their metal helmets gleaming in the morning sun. They followed behind Ubel and my companions. I turned away and faced the hills ahead to avoid looking at him anymore.

I smiled to myself. You just wait, Clod. Afraid that I had said that out loud, I shot a glance toward my companions. Mercifully quiet, the faraway look in their eyes showed them deep in their own minds. Even the small-brained Dog guarded his thoughts.

As for me, my hearty breakfast lay heavy on my stomach as we headed out.

The two gold riders on their silver dragons worried me the most. I could tell the way they circled the silvers before mounting and the haughty manner they looked around when they took to the air that these were not like goofy old Dog. The silvers certainly showed more aggression than Trigger ever thought about as they flew low over the human soldiers. Even when he took me for that first scary ride. These dragon soldiers spared no love for their own kind.

The silvers and their riders circled slowly on the far left and right of the battalion as we marched between the low hills out of town. Within minutes, we followed a route up narrow canyons with hillsides sparsely covered by gnarled trees with few leaves to keep them alive. I led the way most of time since forks in the arroyos and multiple tracks led the men astray. Ubel hated that he couldn't remain in front but after I corrected him five times in as many minutes, he motioned me forward.

"But you'd better not get any wise ideas just because you're leading."

"No sir, I know the easiest and fastest way. You'll see."

A large hill loomed ahead. I glanced right and left and saw that Ubel's dragons circled far away and a little behind the battalion. Good.

This is the one. Go up to the top. It was Skye's voice!

I leaned forward and pumped my legs vigorously as we struggled up the loose sand and rocks, zig-zagging back and forth to make the steep climb more bearable. Reaching the top just ahead of Wyetta who barely breathed hard, I turned and scanned the landscape behind me to make sure the silvers and golds were still behind us. Then I looked to my left. A shadow passed over a dry arroyo in the distance.

I saw the rhythmic rise and fall of dark blue joints, shaped like knobs, draped over with massive sheets of skin. The pulse of dragon wings! Skye and Caerulus flew slightly below the horizon of low hills to the west. Before Ubel reached the top, followed closely by Clod, the two blue dragons swooped upwards. They grabbed air with their wings then leveled and sped at us faster than I've ever seen dragons fly. I spun around, latched onto Wyetta's shoulder and pulled her face down into the sand of the hilltop.

I squatted and shouted, "Down, Tristram or lose your head!"

For a moment, he looked at me, confused, then darted his head left and hit the ground. At the same time Wyetta dug her nails into my arm, yelling obscenities, but she choked her voice off when the two dragons flew right over us. They dipped left and knocked down the first ten or more soldiers that clamored up behind us. Clod pulled out a short sword, swung and missed the pair of dragons as they flew away.

Right behind them, eight dragons approached along the same path, but they quickly split up and glided down the hill knocking soldiers right and left with their claws balled up like fists. A pair of the blues split farther apart headed for Ubel's dragons who were now flapping their wings frantically in our direction.

A stunning scene spread out in front of me. Glittering helmets flew in all directions. None of the soldiers had a chance to raise their javelins. Six dragons circled toward each other, then dropped steeply and unleashed a curtain of flame over the soldiers farther down the hill.

Meanwhile, the other pair of blues met the silvers and golds, shooting quick bursts of flame in their direction. At first, Ubel's dragons deftly dipped and darted away from the flames but they couldn't overcome the wash of air the big blues' wings pushed toward them. Both pairs flailed trying to right themselves and avoid slamming into the hilltops. But they failed and each slammed into the sand, the clouds of dirt quickly overwhelmed by wide spouts of flame the blues shot at them.

Even at a few hundred yards away, I heard the smaller dragons scream.

As if I had something to do with the onslaught, I raised both fists and shouted "Hooray! Fry 'em mighty dragons! Show them who the real warriors are!"

As if to answer my rashness, a club hit the back of my head knocking me down the hill. As I rolled, I twisted around and saw that Ubel had hit me with a short wooden baton. Dang! I had not kept my eye on him when the attack started.

No time for regrets, I turned and rolled away from the glut of soldiers down the hill from me. Now beyond their reach, a few raised their crossbows and aimed at me. I couldn't tell if they had shot their bolts, but if they did, they missed.

I got little comfort in that because the ground dropped off the edge of the hill in front of me. I feared I couldn't stop my slide down the hill. Still on my belly, I plowed my elbows into the ground and headed into a mass of rocks at the edge of the cliff.

That slowed me enough that I spun around and dug my heels into the rocks, stopping short of flying off the ten-foot-high cliff.

I looked back up to see Ubel swinging his iron baton . He ordered his soldiers to raise their pikes and javelins as a dragon knocked them all, including Ubel, off their feet. Now several of them skidded down my way. I rolled away from the cliff's edge but two other soldiers ran over me as they climbed up the hill. Suddenly Wyetta rushed downhill toward me, taking long steps, digging in her heels to keep her descent under control. She snatched a baton from a man near her and swung it wide at the two soldiers who had me at their feet. They flew off in opposite directions, swallowed by the mass of men just below.

Farther down the hill, the airborne dragons lit up the rest of the battalion. Men ran into each other in their frantic efforts to extinguish the flames that engulfed them. A horrid sight for sure, but somehow, I felt no need to wish mercy on them.

Above, more dragons flew into sight as they spread out to aim thin streams of fire at those soldiers who managed to separate themselves from the flaming masses below me. More those men from above fell toward me, rolling past

Wyetta, two of them knocking my feet out of the rock pile that kept me from flying off the cliff.

Wyetta grabbed at me, but she couldn't reach me. Was this it? Will I fly into space and shatter into pieces while she watched? A flash of silver came at me like a bolt of lightning.

Grab on, human!

"Trigger! What are you doing?"

He swung under me as my feet broke free of the crumbling ground. No time to think or aim, I grasped with both arms at the flash of silver in front of me. My right hand hit a spine as my left hand immediately grasped the other side of that spine. I sensed Trigger shifting his position in mid-air when he came under me and then ascended hard, right between my legs.

Lord and Creator! That hurt in the last place where guys don't want to get kicked, but I held firm while I screamed bloody murder. If I had a breath left in me, I would have cussed a blue and silver streak, but all I could do was hang on and lean against that crazy silver as he flew straight up and banked right, avoiding flaming blues right, left, above and below.

My head cleared. I looked down and saw Wyetta thread her way around the rim of the cliff to escape the flames. Soldiers flailed widely in all directions trying to hit the diving dragons and Tristram as he struggled to follow Wyetta away from the attacking men.

"Trigger, I don't know about you. You're the last dragon I would have expected here, but I'm dad-blamed glad you tagged along. You and I got off to a bad start, but maybe we can work something out."

Later for that, human. Look below. Your new human leader still lives.

Sure enough, Ubel had managed to flatten himself on top of the hill enough to avoid the claws and wings of any dragons flying overhead. In the melee, he worked his way toward Tristram.

I yelled, "Drop down, Trigger!" But the silver didn't change course. I leaned over and called out to the old man. "Tristram! Behind you! Ubel!"

He turned in confusion just as Ubel slammed his baton into the side of the old man's head. Tristram fell like a sack of rocks.

"No!" I cried. "Take me down, now, Trigger, slam it! I need to help my friend."

Trigger hesitated as two blues sped below us, then he dipped straight down to quickly level out and land with a thud. On my right, Ubel stood over Tristram as he threw down his baton and clutched his sword at his waist. I jumped off Trigger. Out of the corner of my eye, I saw Wyetta clamoring up the hill. I reached down to a fallen soldier at my feet, picked up his crossbow, raised it and pulled the trigger. The bolt flew fifteen feet in an instant to hit right between Ubel's eyes. Blood flew out as if boiling out of a cauldron.

"Yes!" I whooped and turned to Wyetta. "Did you see that? I couldn't have taken my time and aimed any better."

She looked at me grimly. "That's great. But you can think about that later. Right now, let's get off this hill down the far side. Those dragons aren't going to spare us any mercy because we're all part of the enemy."

"Nope! We're good. Let's get off the hill. We'll be fine. You'll see." I turned to Trigger and asked, "Can you carry two?"

If I have to. Get her on. Hurry!

I motioned to Wyetta to climb behind me. With a mixture of fear and doubt on her face, she climbed on. Trigger rose more slowly and poured his energy into working our way through the marauding blue dragons. "Lay down, Wyetta!" I called out.

We flattened ourselves against Trigger to avoid the massive blue wings flapping all around us while I heard a frantic cackling. I looked behind us for a moment and saw little Dog flying low. I had forgotten about him!

"Come on, little guy. Follow us and stay close. You'll be OK, dragons surround us! No better place to be." I laughed more like a maniac as I gripped Wyetta's hands to put her arms around me.

She cursed, "Blamed dragons, what are they doing? How did they know?"

We reached the shady side of the hill where it was quieter. Without having me say anything, Trigger landed gently and I plopped off to take stock of my body to check for damages. Faint but sharp pains all over my head, back, arms, and chest jabbed at my consciousness. It was no use because everything darkened as if a cloud passed in front of the sun.

Oh no, I couldn't pass out now.

Wyetta looked all around us. No one stood on top of the hill. The sounds of battle seemed quieter than just moments before. "You're right. They're not interested in us. The dragons are just attacking our captors. What is this?"

"You'll see. In good time, you'll see."

Dog flitted down next to me and looked at Wyetta and then me.

Crazy! Big dragons! Wild men! Poor Dog! You save. Many thanks!

I barely heard his last words when the entire world grew ever darker as I faded out.

EIGHTEEN

The Quiet After Battle

Dreams of fires burning across my dad's fields and those of our neighbors dogged me for what seemed hours during my restless sleep. Then everything changed and the fields were suddenly filled with men wearing metal helmets. They clashed with each other, striking their comrades with javelins. Overhead, Skye flew low spreading flame like a flood inundating everything under her. She came toward me still spewing flames.

"No! It's me, it's me. Don't burn me!" I cried as I swatted my hand against something thick that restrained my motions. It was my sleeping pad covers. I opened my eyes and saw dim shafts of light against the cave walls in Skye and Caerulus' home. I threw off those clinging covers.

A dream. No, a nightmare. Thank the stars for that small favor. A long silver body lay curled up on the smooth rock floor next to my bed of furs. For a moment, I didn't recognize the silver form until a head about the size of half-grown calf's reared up and turned to me. This was no calf because its mouth wide like a lizard's, the eyes a dark gray, and the plentiful teeth were long and sharp.

Good. You're awake. You sleep noisy, Trigger said.

"So, you've been here all... uh, is it night or day?"

Day. Mid-afternoon. You sleep since yesterday. Only awake now.

"Yikes, over a full day." I slowly stood, struggling against a lot of stiffness. It reminded me of my old grandma complaining about her painful joints. Now I knew what she felt like every morning. I inspected my arms, legs and found I had enough scratches and cuts to last me a lifetime. But nothing seemed beyond healing.

I hobbled into the main room of the cave and found it empty. Trigger and I seemed to be the only ones home.

"Where is everyone?"

Woman and old man with Owyn and Luc. Took the gold to corral with other golds. Gold scared. He ate, slept alone. Skye and Caerulus gone to get Baldric.

"Gol-darned, that was quick. I hope they get him back all right." Beat up and half awake, I didn't think any more about Skye and Caerulus. After a short time, I didn't remember what Trigger told me. Crazy.

"All right, thanks. I'll check on Dog—that's the gold's name—but right now I want to see how the old man is doing. Is he alive?"

Don't know. Didn't ask. Woman didn't sleep until late. She watched us. Didn't say anything. Talked to herself. Looked all over Novis. Stared at the desert. She not see desert before? Don't like her. Why you bring her?

"She was a prisoner with me. Seems like she knows a lot about dragons. She is very tough, so I wouldn't mess with her like you did with me."

Trigger gave me a look like, "Who me? Little ol' innocent me?" He didn't actually say anything, but he didn't need to.

"Let's go see her," I said.

You go. I go see gold. Dog? Funny dragon name, even for a gold.

"I think he's been treated badly and maybe he's not all there." I pointed to my head to indicate he either wasn't too bright or he was a little crazy.

Trigger just gave me a blank look like he didn't understand. Maybe he didn't, but I had the feeling he always played a little dumber so he could have the upper hand when he needed it.

Without another word, I headed for Owyn and Luc's cave while Trigger flew off to the corral. Needless to say, I didn't find her, so I just visited with the two dragon brothers and got the gory details of the battle from their point of view.

Yeah, Owyn said, *we had fun getting to use our flame for the first time in battle! I couldn't believe how easy I fried those dumb humans. I wish they would bathe or something because burning those bodies smelled pretty bad! My brother and I had the same problem being around them when they kept us captive. Their odor, pew!*

Luc let out something like a growling laugh, though most wouldn't think he laughed. I could tell by the sparkle of his eyes, he had great fun burning those men.

Luc said, *I got to sharpen my aim when I burned a few of their long sticks.*

"Those are called javelins," I said. "That's all these guys had a chance to use for weapons. I don't know why they couldn't put the long pikes into action to stab you and I don't think any of them even had whips to beat you since that's how the dragon train handlers control dragons. Maybe they wanted to travel light with weapons that were quicker to move around in battle.

"My dad had his pike from the old Dragon Wars that he just leaned up against the wall in the barn. "I tried to take it outside one time and poke around with it in the corral, but it was so long and heavy, I could barely budge it. Dropped it on the floor and it took everything I had to lean it back up. The next morning Dad noticed it had been moved. He gave me a look and grunted. Figured I probably learned not to mess with a man's weapon. He only pointed his finger at me and said, 'Punk!' Anyway, that's neither here nor there, I want to see my friend Tristram—the old man—and see how's he's doing."

Go on back, Luc said and nodded at a small entrance to a back room in their cave. Both brothers stayed put and let me go in alone.

I sat next to poor old Tristram who looked like he had been beaten within an inch of his long life. The only way I knew he lived was his ragged breath that followed each slow heave of his chest.

I said dumb things, wondering if he could hear me or not. "I bet you're ready to feel better and get up and enjoy your new freedom. Don't be scared by Owyn and Luc. They're good dragons and they'll make sure you're all right. I'll bring around some food when you're ready to eat something. It won't be much, but it won't be rotten or moldy, either."

His breathing smoothed out a little and sounded more like he rested instead of suffering from the beating he had taken. Maybe he'd be all right after all.

I chatted with the brothers a little longer and then left looking for Wyetta. I wondered what she was searching for. I could tell Trigger didn't like her wandering around, but when I first came here, that's what I did. No other humans had seen a village of dragons before. Dragons at peace of all things.

I found her near the hill where the corral was located.

"Hi, Wyetta, how do you feel?"

She greeted me with a wide smile and strode toward me like I was a long-lost friend. She spread her arms wide and gave me a hardy hug.

"Whoa! That's kind of a strong hug! Did you miss me that much?" I said, rather stunned by her familiarity. Was that a special hug?

"Just glad to see you up and out." She stared at my face and inspected my arms, legs, and neck. "You look like the demons worked you over before spitting you out of the pits of Hades!" She laughed. "And they did. First in that *wonderful palace* with Ubel and then the beating we took during the big battle yesterday."

I looked at her carefully, though not boldly like she looked me over. "Well, I can see you've been in a scuffle, but I'm amazed how well you look. Beautiful."

And she was. Her tall, lean body, bright smiling face, and flowing blond hair made her the most beautiful woman I had ever seen. The past several days in prison, traveling in the dragon train, and then yesterday's battle hadn't given me much of chance to admire her. She certainly didn't have much chance to look her best.

But standing in front of me, just the two of us, she was the most pleasant sight I'd ever seen. Though I wasn't much of an expert with the young ladies, at that moment I felt I might have a chance to get her interested in me. But I had to be careful not to say something stupid, like calling her beautiful like I had just done.

"Thanks," she said as if she heard that sort of thing every day. Which she probably did. Always unsure of myself, only one drawback occurred to me. She was at least three or four years older than me.

Oh well...

"Come on," I said, "let's go back to Skye and Caerulus' cave and I'll tell you a little bit about Novis, this village of newly free dragons."

She looked at me like I was a little nuts. "Who are Skye and Car, uh Carully? And what is Novis? Are there some people here I haven't met yet?"

"No, uh. Hmm. You misunderstand. Skye and *Caerulus*—that's how you say his name—are the blue dragons that led the attack yesterday. I, uh, you know, I knew they were ready to attack if and when I came back..."

I didn't know what to do at that moment because I had just mouthed off too much. This wasn't a good time to reveal that the dragons and I talked to each other. There would be a time for that. Right then, she seemed so confused and, what was that word my teacher would use about some of the kids who learned more slowly?

Clueless. Yes, that's it. So was I for saying too much.

Wyetta normally came across as confident and bold. More like a well-trained soldier than a woman of about twenty or twenty-one. At least not like the women that age in Hilltop. But with this, she seemed clueless about how dragons really were.

But then how could she know? Sure, she said she had been around dragons and all, but I was pretty sure she didn't hear their thoughts like I did. The day I first met Skye, I heard what she said in my head, while everyone else in the village only heard funny noises. They certainly didn't hear words.

Wyetta was definitely a dragon lover like those vile people in the prison and the train people called us. But maybe for her, it was different. She also had strong feelings about how badly dragons were treated. I was sure, soon, she would hear their thoughts and realize she could talk to them. But I decided to say no more about it because I didn't think I had the right to give away secrets about the dragons to someone I barely knew.

That would be up to them, not me.

She smiled broadly, flashing those perfect teeth at me. "I'm so glad to see you getting better," she said. "Never mind about these dragons. They're amazing fighters. Hard to believe they lost the Dragon Wars to people all those years ago. But maybe they can get their freedom back, huh?"

"Yeah..."

"And being quite the farmer boy, uh, man, you know a thing or two about animals and, shall we say, beasts. So, I'll go along with whatever you say. But I would be interested in knowing more about how they got themselves ready to ambush us, you know, Ubel and his soldiers. And, that other soldier that got really pushy with you in the battle. You called him, Club—"

"Clod. Yes! I forgot about him. I didn't see him after the dragons attacked. I guess he got burned in the melee. At least, I hope so... Say, I'd like to go back to the battleground and see if I can find his body."

She frowned. "I don't think that's a good idea. By now the people from Lynden have heard about the battle and they'll be swarming all over those hills like ants. So, do you think the dragons can make this kind of attack all over again? Are there more dragons?"

"I..." What could I do? For very selfish reasons, I
didn't want to say any more about the dragons and my
special friendship with them. Did I really want to share
Skye, her family and all the rest of the dragons, even big,
scary Hellmuth with her or anyone else?

I didn't know at that point. I needed to think and I
needed to talk to Skye. Where was she? And Caerulus?
There was something someone said about them earlier,
but what was it? Right at that point, my head was still
pretty mixed up after that battle. To make it worse, I felt
very alone and uneasy.

At that moment, I realized that old Tristram must be
just what he said. And not a spy for Ubel. The same with
Wyetta. But I didn't want to say or do anything more
until I talked to my closest friend in the world, Skye.

It hurt when she got mad at me when I first contacted
her on the way to Lynden when the dragon train reached
the high point past Hilltop. But I couldn't blame her since
I didn't bring back Baldric. As I walked along in silence
with Wyetta, I thought back about that conversation I had
with Skye. Maybe I could spot things I had said that
made her so upset with me. I had tried really hard to send
my thoughts to her when the train passed Hilltop.

I remember I waited until I could actually look out on the
brown and tan desert at the edge of the northern lands
before I contacted Skye. Miles and miles away, I stood on
tiptoes looking over the wall at the front of our train car.
Maybe she could hear my thoughts easier if I gazed at the
lands where she was.

I concentrated like never before. Then I sensed something, maybe whispering. It sounded like Skye.

Jaiden? Is that you? I can barely hear something in my head. If that's you, try again.

'I had given up contacting you. I am so far away. Remember the deep valley just north of Hilltop? We're now going down into that valley. It will be another couple of days at this rate before we reach Lynden. And then we will walk north toward Septrion.'

We? Who's we?

'Oh. Well, that's a long story. Right now, you need to gather all the dragons who are ready for battle. I'm on one of three trains loaded with human soldiers and weapons coming your way to Novis and on to the Founders if they're not stopped.'

The silence that followed, worse than the silence when I first tried to contact Baldric, became frightful while I quickly explained my situation, what I did, and why.

Then… I swear, in my head, my entire body shook from Skye's roar that could have brought down the fortress in Portville. Thank the Creator that it wasn't an actual sound because I would have been struck deaf and my body melted into a pile of goo from the vibrations.

'So, when you calm down, I'll tell you what I have in mind and then you can tell me how you, Caerulus and all the rest of the dragons are going to deal with this.'

After I explained my idea, Skye replied in a voice very calm but as cold as ice. *You will do what you have said. I will monitor your arrival in Lynden without any humans seeing me. Now that we can communicate over a long distance, that will be easier. You will remain calm and be*

prepared to move quickly and precisely as I have ordered.
You will share my orders with your companions or they,
too, will find themselves dead before they know what hits
them.

Am I clear?

'Very. I know this is not the way any of you wanted to
start this whole big... thing. But it's the best I could do
and hope to stay alive and be of some use. I only wish I
could have brought Baldric, but I couldn't think of a—'

No! It is best he remains in the Big Barn. He has a
chance to survive for now, but once this starts, he will be
in danger. Caerulus will know what to do. I wish I could
take you right now with me to tell this news to him so you
could feel his fury, if not his flame.

'I'll just imagine it. Thank you very much.'

I waited a few moments.

'Is that all?'

For now. Sleep well when you get to Lynden. You will
need it.

'Yes, ma'am. Bye for now.'

For now.

I sighed and returned to the present and looked for a place
to sit down because the memory of our talk and how cold
she sounded made me lightheaded. Of course, I never had
the chance to warn my companions of the ambush, but
somehow that turned out all right anyway, except I did
worry about old Tristram.

Anyway, I didn't want to collapse and look like a fool
in front of Wyetta or anyone else for that matter after
passing out following the battle the day before.

"Are you all right?" Wyetta asked.

"Yeah. I think I've been on my feet a little too much and haven't recovered from the battle. Just give me a few moments. Go on and look around some more, if you want."

She looked at me like I had rejected her or something. "Are you sure?"

"Yes. Whatever you want to do. I need a little quiet for now."

"Sounds like a good idea. Maybe I should take a nap myself. I'm always getting up and at 'em too quickly my, uh, father always says. So... see you later."

She went off toward Luc and Owyn's cave. I wondered what it felt like to be in a cave alone with two dragons and none of them talking to each other. At least between the brothers and this strange human female.

As I sat, a crazy realization popped in my head. Great Creator, Skye and Caerulus are on their way to rescue Baldric! When I heard that earlier, it just went right over my bleary head. Now, the danger they faced suddenly swept over me. Why didn't anyone stop them?

And then another crazy thought. Maybe I should go fast as I can to Portville and help get Baldric out of there. I could—

No. Stupid idea. But then, how could I make things any worse than they already were? I wonder if Trigger could get me there in time?

And what about those three boys we helped to escape the Big Barn a couple of years ago when Skye, her family, and I had taken off? Those guys really knew the Barn and dragons well and could get me in there with them so we could—somehow—get Baldric out. I didn't think Skye and Caerulus could just fly in there and scoop him up. Not without getting a whole gang of handlers on their tails. The handlers could wrap their whips around the dragons' necks and chain those two blues to the floor in minutes. And what if there were soldiers there guarding Baldric?

I had to go. No matter how stupid I might be, I had a better chance with help from those three guys to find Baldric and get him out.

At least, I hoped so.

NINETEEN

Into the Black Hole

I grabbed my slingshot and packed it in the leather pouch on my belt that was among my stuff at Azure Den before heading for the corral to find Trigger. I began to think about Thanos, the other silver that messed up allowing Skye and Caerulus' children to be stolen. Was he so innocent? For some reason, I felt like Trigger didn't do anything bad. Could I assume that about Thanos?

Things just kept turning around on me in ways I didn't expect. Everything was just so uncertain.

Anyway, Skye had said Thanos took other silvers with him to keep an eye on Lynden after Ubel's soldiers headed north. No one wanted escaping soldiers to return to Lynden and alert the town about the ambush.

But who knew if those silvers were still on duty near Lynden? I wondered if they got caught. Catching silvers would probably be easier for the townspeople than catching big blues who could torch them in moments. Still, that wasn't as important as heading south to help Skye.

I realized Hellmuth and the others wouldn't exactly be happy to find me gone if I took off for Portville riding Trigger. So, I resolved, as scary as it might be, to let him know. I had already pushed my luck too far with Skye.

At the corral, I found Trigger with Dog.

Dog better now, Trigger said. *Likes the food and other golds. Ubel scared him. Beat him. Dog now happy.*

Dog twisted himself around my feet with excitement. *Dog happy. Stay here. Hate fortress.*

"Glad to hear it." I turned my attention back to Trigger. "Look, we need to fly south to the Big Barn in Portville. Do you know the way?"

Big Barn my home. I didn't like it. But... can find it in my sleep.

"Good. We need to get there ahead of Skye and Caerulus so they don't get caught trying to rescue Baldric."

I like Baldric. Will do anything to help. I know quick way. Silvers are faster than big, slow blues. Let's go!

"We will, but first I have to tell Hellmuth that—"

Jaiden crazy. Hellmuth eat you for lunch!

"I'll have to take that chance. But after all that's happened, he should know what we're going to do because it'll cause all Hades to break loose if we charge in and take Baldric."

The silver looked at me, his eyes frowned and he blew out a harsh breath. I believe he thought he was looking at a dead man.

"You're probably right, it's stupid and Hellmuth will fry me on the spot. But I would rather die fast than see what manure I stirred up if I sneaked away."

You will die. I stay here. You come back if you live.

"Well, that's an idea, but I don't want to waste time. Fly me to his cave in the Founders village and I'll face him alone."

Nice knowing you. All right, I take dead man to Hellmuth.

He took me, not to the cave entrance, but to the edge of a small pond fed by water from the Rio Roho.

That way to Hellmuth, Trigger said as he pointed with the tip of his tail.

The entrance to the leader's cave was guarded by Dracul, the old blue who had trained me earlier.

"I seek time with Hellmuth to talk about Skye and Caerulus' rescue flight to Portville."

Dracul stepped toward me, leaned down and gazed into my eyes. The smell of sulfur nearly knocked me flat. His eyes, flecked with dark spots and film like an old dog's, regarded me like I was a pile of fresh meat.

"It won't take long," I said. "I don't want to disturb him but I must. Please?"

The old dragon straightened up and smiled. *This I have to see. I didn't train you for this sort of thing.*

He lumbered into the cave. After more time than I could afford, he came back out. *Enter. He will see you.*

As I walked into the dark entrance, I couldn't see anything but the vague outlines of walls that reached high beyond my poor vision. A spot of light off to my right entered from a small hole in the ceiling. The dragon motioned me to sit on a large bench in front of a larger bench opposite.

I didn't know if I should sit or stand, but in a moment, Hellmuth entered, his head brushing the ceiling. I knew he was big from the Council of Dragons, but now in the confines of this cave, he appeared even more gigantic. He sat on the larger bench, tucking all four of his legs underneath his belly. He didn't offer me the other one, so I stood.

I have very little time for this. A storm from the south approaches, so tell me what's on your mind and quickly leave me to my plans.

I was pretty sure he wasn't talking about the weather in the south. But the time had come for me, ready or not.

"I want to help Skye and Caerulus get Baldric out of the Big Barn. Trigger knows the way and will take me. He says he's faster than the two blue dragons so I could get there and offer my help before they attack. I don't think they can simply take their son from the humans holding him. I can sneak in with some help, find Baldric and get him out."

You're a fool and you will end up a dead fool!

"I know that's possible but there are too many dragon handlers—not to mention cannons—for my two friends to overcome and get Baldric out safely. I have a better chance, though I know, not a great one. I would rather die trying than keep feeling I failed Skye when they took Baldric in Lynden."

You did save the other two. Skye told me of your earlier bravery. But this is stupidity, not courage.

"I know, but like I said—"

Crazy stubborn human! Hellmuth roared.

He stood and stamped around like he was getting ready to crush me. Instead, he leaned over and looked me in the eye. Unlike Dracul, his eyes were the size of a big bull's head and as clear as the stream near our house before winter froze it solid. The golden flecks in his eyes danced and spun reflecting back the single bright light from the hole in the ceiling.

I may be crazy but I had a hunch he was reading every thought I've ever had. Is that possible?

He flashed me a frightening grin. *Go kill yourself but try to keep Skye and Caerulus alive so they can return for the battles to come. I would prefer you to keep Trigger safe, too. We'll need him also.*

"It'll just be me in the Big Barn. If I die, I die alone surrounded by dragon-hating humans."

I sounded a lot braver and sure of myself than I really was. I had to convince him I would not lead my two blue friends to their death. Or the silver, either. Just me putting my head on the chopping block.

Fine. Leave, I'm busy.

He turned and stomped away. He stopped just before he went out of sight. He looked at me over his shoulder.

May the Dragons of the Heavens be with you, foolish young man.

And he was gone.

Young man! Not boy. That was something. Maybe enough to push me toward this fool's mission. I really didn't want to die. Really, really didn't want to. But I couldn't live with myself if I didn't do this.

As I left, I spoke to Dracul. "I want to thank you for your training. It kept me alive and I was able to fool Ubel."

He grunted and nodded. "You're braver than I thought, so I also wish the Dragons Above go with you."

Outside, I ran to Trigger whose raised arches over his eyes showed surprise I was still alive.

"He and Dracul wished the Dragons of Heaven to go with me. You, too, I imagine. But he wants me to make sure you and my two friends stay alive."

Fine with me. Let's go.

The silver was right. He could fly way faster than Skye. I couldn't hang on tight enough so I made him slow down and fly low over the hills near Lynden. There had to be farms around the town and where there were farms, there were saddles and leather.

Sure enough, I spied a nice big barn over a hill south of Lynden. We landed in a small grove of scrub oak bushes at the end of the field. With no one around, I snuck up to the barn and let myself into its darkness. Ah, the smell of dried manure and straw.

Though not as dark as Hellmuth's cave, it was almost as big. I found a tack room giving me a choice of a small saddle for a pony or a large one for a field horse. I found a set of reins used for the hay wagon, several strips of leather and a sharp knife. With the small saddle, knife and plenty of leather, I backtracked to Trigger.

Look at that! Jaiden, good thief.

The saddle didn't fit between Trigger's spines, so I had to forget that plan. I took the wide strips of leather, cut them to the length I needed, and wound them around Trigger several times and then around my waist and legs. I finished by wrapping my hands with the ends of the strips. I think I overdid it, but I didn't want to fall several hundred feet over the mountains as Trigger flew southeast toward Portville. I tucked the reins under me and stashed the knife in my pouch.

We took off. The cold wind stole my breath, but we had to get there before the two blues tried to enter the Barn. The landscape below changed from gnarly hills to an area greener than Lynden but nothing like the lush valleys of Hilltop.

Next stop, a village in the middle of a rocky area with low hills. It had been over two years since I first flew over the small farms of this area. They were rather bare compared to our farms in Hilltop like I remembered but it didn't look right somehow.

"Trigger, could you circle around and fly over this area from the southwest?"

He turned head around and looked at me. *Why?*

"I don't recognize the village below because I flew over it from the opposite direction. Just do it. Hurry."

Yes, whatever.

Then it started to look like the fuzzy memory I had in my head. "Down there just past those houses on the other side of the hill. If you see anyone, keep going." He didn't see anyone so we landed. I walked over the hill to near a house that looked familiar. A boy approached me from a weathered outbuilding.

"What can I do for you?" he asked, though not in a friendly manner.

"I'm looking for an old friend from my days in Portville..." I just realized that I had forgotten the so-called old friend's name. I struggled to jog my memory.

The boy smiled. "You look like you're about the same age as my brother. He was in Portville. He worked in, uh, this big place. I can't remember—"

"Was it the Big Barn?"

"Yes, that's it. Are you Jaiden?"

I was stunned the kid knew my name. I must have the right place. Right then, it was confirmed when a lanky guy about my age strolled out of the farmhouse. "Jaiden! Look at you!"

As soon as I saw him, his name came to me. "Altan! I don't believe it. You're still all in one piece. I guess the train people didn't come around looking for you."

"Oh, they did," he said as he approached me and stuck out his hand. I gripped his hand, glad to see a familiar face from a time almost as scary as what I faced right then. "They came around asking my parents and young brother all kinds of questions. But my family just said they didn't know anything." He laughed. "My father said I never came back home and it was good riddance because they couldn't stand to have a dragon lover under their roof."

Altan's brother chuckled, too. "Yeah, too bad. All he does is give me grief just because he's my smartass older brother." They punched each other playfully.

"Come on in," Altan said.

"Let me talk to you privately. I've got a problem and I need your help."

"Anything you have to say can be said in front of my parents and baby brother."

So, once inside their home, I explained why I was heading back to Portville and needed his help to get in the Big Barn.

"I'll go—"

"No, son don't!" his mother said. "I won't let you go back there."

"A time's coming when we can't hold back, Ma. This has gone on too long," Altan said.

His father nodded. "He's right, Mother. It's the least we can do the way those hot shots in Portville push us around. They leave us out here without any roads to take our produce into the big city to sell or even to the larger towns around here. We can't be free until the dragons are."

Altan's mother stuck her jaw out and gave her husband a stern look. "What good is freedom if our son is dead? There are others—"

"But others aren't me," Altan protested. "How can I hold my head up if I stayed behind because my mother didn't want me to take a risk?" He gave his mother the same stern look she had given his father. "I'm my father's *and* my mother's son. I know you wouldn't back down if I was threatened. It's the same with me. I'm growing up, I have to do something to protect my family. Those in Portville will never let up on us unless we stand up to them."

He turned to his father, his eyebrows raised as if asking for more support. His father nodded to him and then faced his wife. "The dragons used to protect farmers when they traveled to bigger towns to sell their produce and meat." He then faced me. "So, the farmers provided food for the dragons that used to live in these hills. That way, the dragons didn't have to prey on people."

Now I understood what inspired such loyalty to dragons out on these rocky hills. My father never mentioned such a thing, but then he didn't say a lot of things to me. I wanted to know more but there was no time for stories or questions.

I turned to Altan. "I sure could use your help. And," I turned to his mother and father, "I will do all I can to keep him from getting caught or hurt by the dragon handlers. I promise."

Now why did I say that? I was glad Trigger was a long way off behind the hill so I wouldn't have to hear his scoffing and complaints.

Now, even his mother's face softened a little when she gave me a quick nod.

We left as soon as we could. Trigger was surprised to see I had Altan with me.

Another crazy human!

I showed Altan how to wrap himself with leather straps to stay on top of the silver. Soon, we were off. We made a quick stop in the next village where Altan easily talked his old buddies, Mamun and Fitzwater, to join us. Fitzwater had grown to be even bigger than he was the last time I saw him. Trigger was not happy.

Four boys on my back—

"Four young men!" I corrected.

Four Idiot men on my back. How can I fly? You wanted speed!

"I know you can do it. I'll bring really good dragon food from the Big Barn for you as a reward."

Sure, you will. You are crazy! I am crazy to be with you.

"Enough! Let's fly."

And we did. Wasn't as fast, but Trigger reached the big water of the east and then rode updrafts from the coastline winds to speed us along.

You are lucky. Winds in our favor. Later in year, not in our favor. Stupid lucky Jaiden!

When he said that last part, I sensed a little good humor in the cranky silver's thoughts. He had to trust my luck and I had to keep that luck in mind when I entered the Big Barn in a few hours.

We came in sight of the big city and saw waves creeping across the coast and crashing into rocks and sandy beaches. As we circled the coast near the Big Barn, I sent my thoughts out to find Skye.

'Are you there?' I thought hard and deep. 'This is Jaiden. You can get mad at me again because I'm just outside Portville flying above the waves with Trigger. You and your mate cannot go into that Big Barn without setting off a disaster. I have help with me. We'll get Baldric and you can take us all home.'

Nothing. Not even a rumble of that same anger I sensed when I first contacted her from the dragon train to Lynden.

I repeated my message again. Then....

Jaiden! We aren't there yet. We've just arrived a few miles away from the Big Barn. How did you get ahead of us?

'Trigger's a fast flyer. I'll explain everything. Where can we meet?'

She suggested a place in a deep valley near the dragon train railroad where dragons learned how to tow a train. I repeated her directions to Trigger.

I know that place. I trained with golds close by. Thick forest. Can't move through when we land.

"Just go," I said out loud. "We'll figure something out when we get there. Maybe Skye knows of a way—"

"Who are you talking to?" Altan yelled.

"Oh. I forgot. I guess there's something you need to know. It's something weird I can do with dragons."

And so, with these guys I decided to take a chance and explain the whole talking-to-dragons thing—why couldn't I do that with Wyetta? Anyway, all three guys were stunned. But it made sense to them when they realized the dragons they knew were always around people. Only they weren't sure why *they* couldn't hear dragons talk in their heads.

"Don't know, guys, but there it is. That's how I knew so much about Caerulus and Skye and their children."

Soon, we approached the area Skye mentioned. I immediately heard her voice in my head. *Continue over the valley below. Now drop down in the thicket of bushes below you. Look for a dark hole in the middle of the thicket. And by the way, Caerulus says you were right to trust these boys about the way you talk to us.*

Well, good. I finally did something right and I barely thought about it before I did it. But I still didn't like Skye knowing my thoughts. I wish I could keep them to myself.

I see the hole, Trigger said, interrupting my thoughts.

Fly into the hole and immediately stop, Skye said. *Tell the boys to duck their heads, it's a tight fit.*

"Hug the silver close and don't raise your heads, guys," I called out. They followed suit as we dropped and flew into a black hole. Somehow the silver stopped just as we slammed into the unseen ground. It wasn't too hard of a landing, yet enough to give everyone a bloody nose as our faces hit Trigger's back.

Jaiden crazy. Skye crazy. Anyone not crazy? he complained.

In the pitch dark we all unwound the leather straps and stumbled around on the uneven ground before I heard a soft rumble.

It's Caerulus, he said. *I'll keep making noises so you can come to us.* His guttural sounds continued and we made our way, tripping every couple of steps until we entered a low open area with a canopy of branches above us. The sun filtered through just enough that we could see our way around as if we were outside walking in the moonlight.

Welcome to our hideaway, Skye said without much emotion.

I wish I could say it was a pleasant reunion, but it wasn't. Of course, both dragons were polite to my companions and even grumpy Trigger. But when it came to me, not so gentle.

How could you be so stupid? This is getting to be a bad habit! Caerulus roared, both in my head and with a growl in his throat. The three guys ducked their heads and cried out. *Sorry,* Caerulus said. *Tell them I'm not mad at them.*

"Fine. Guys, that was meant for me, not you. I have a talent for making Caerulus, and now, Skye mad at me." I turned back to the two sulking dragons, "Anyway, just think about what kind of trouble you two would stir up waltzing into the Big Barn to rescue your boy? Not real good, huh?"

Perhaps not. Caerulus grumbled.

"No. It would be an instant declaration of war and they would bring out all the whips, long halberds—you know, the poles with sharp blades on the ends—not to mention their cannons! I mean, what do you think they would do? Invite you in for tea?"

No, you're right, Skye admitted. *It would be war.*

Suddenly, I noticed a radical shift in her mood as a storm of dragon language between her and Caerulus shot through my mind in a fury.

Then she turned to me and broke out the widest dragon smile I had seen yet.

It would be war but instead here's what we're going to do....

TWENTY

Return to the Big Barn

The next morning, well before sunrise, four humans and three dragons slowly came alive. After the long flight and stumbling around in the Black Hole area, the guys and I still felt beat up. Yet we were anxious to put Skye's plan into action. Trigger must have been tired, too, carrying three extra people but he pretended to be fine. The blue dragons acted like this was a stroll through the meadow but I had my doubts. After all, it was their oldest son we were going to rescue or get us all killed trying.

The night before, I climbed out of our hideaway and found wild fruits and dug up tubers to eat. With Altan, Mamun and Fitzwater's help we cornered several fat rabbits for the dragons and us to snack on. No big game hunting for now.

At least both Skye and her mate could cook our food. Without any seasoning, supper tasted pretty bland if not a little bitter, but it filled our stomachs. A nearby stream helped ease our thirst. Cups of hot tea were only a daydream for now. We had enough left over for a quick breakfast courtesy of Caerulus reheating it for us.

While we ate, Skye and I had a private conversation.

'I'm sorry I messed up things so bad trying to rescue your young ones and then the big fight outside Lynden all while leaving Baldric behind,' I said in my thoughts to her. 'But there was no way to get him free.'

Of course. I thought I already reassured you about all of that business right after your rescue attempt. And that battle with Ubel's men was almost too easy but those so-called soldiers were only guards from the fortress which is run by the Dragon Train Company. The real soldiers of the Dear Leader in Portville are considerably more able and lethal. They have learned a lot and now they have cannons. Any real war will be much worse than the Dragon Wars back in the old days.

'Think Hellmuth has some new ideas?'

I'm sure he does and so do those of us who have seen the weapons of the human armies we've transported around the entire countryside in the last few years.

'Where are all those armies?'

Spread all over the domain. But somewhere in the far western lands there is a big town or an area called Westin, beyond the edge of Emerald Forest. I've heard rumors that some kind of major complex of fortresses is in Westin. Some of us train dragons have taken supplies and men out there, but then we left them in various small towns along the edge of a sparse forest of small trees called the Deadly Plains.

'That name tells you a lot, doesn't it?'

I'm not sure if that's just a name passed around among the soldiers or it's a real name, but it has to be big because the towns where men, supplies, and weapons have been taken are not big enough to support such quantities. No dragons have seen Westin or the actual fortresses.

'Maybe they will leave the dragons in peace.'

That's what we thought—no, it's what we hoped for. But the kidnapping of our children, the movement of Ubel's unprepared soldiers north of Lynden, and clamping down on humans who don't want war with dragons—

'Yeah, dragon lovers like me!'

Yes. They are all signs of what is to come. I'm glad you are here. I've missed you since you were taken prisoner with Baldric. I feel responsible for you, but now I see you are ready to take part. So, what do you think of my plans— or I should say, our plans?

'I can't think of anything better, so let's get started.'

I got everyone else's attention, swallowed and prayed for courage and, I hope, success.

"Now for the hard part," I said to my human and dragon comrades. "You two blues—" I laughed. "Do you like the sound of 'you two blues'?"

They didn't crack a dragon smile. I went on. "Stay put right here until you hear from me. Meanwhile, after Trigger lets us off, we still have a bit of a hike ahead and have to somehow figure out how to get in the barn and find Baldric. I'll let you know every move we make, but no comments from you two. Especially you, Caerulus. We'll be the ones on the scene, but I can't describe or explain everything we do because we have to focus on whatever comes to hand. My intention is to do what they least expect us to do. Maybe."

Trigger snorted. *Trigger take you now. Come back. Wait. Glad to stay here. Not need human trouble. I fly with the blues. Later.*

Recalling a line from a story we learned in school, I said, "'Today is a good day to die...' or something like that. But here's what I say—It's a better day to stay alive."

Trigger flew us out of the thicket into the dark blue light before dawn. Though it was dim, I saw we were in a rather pleasant valley of huge rocks, tall oaks, and steep cliffs all around. Staying low to the ground, he headed for buildings nearby. He let us down close to two long buildings where the train cars were stored. I watched him fly off, so low to the ground, his wings kicked up dust clouds.

"I hope we're alive to ride home on his back," Mamun said.

"Yeah, he's a feisty one, isn't he?" agreed Fitzwater.

We made our way between buildings to a wide walkway that passed through the north side of the big city. In the distance along the coast, I saw the towers of the stone fortress where I had been captive a few days before. A little inland was the massive wooden block that was the Big Barn.

Altan pointed to the side of the barn facing the fortress a few hundred yards away. "That's our best chance to get in there without too many eyes on us. That is if things are about the same inside."

"Yeah, if," I said. I sighed made my way through a collection of broken-down homes and shacks that sat between the train buildings and the barn. We had poor people in Hilltop who also lived near the tracks. Most worked on some of the farms from time to time to help when big jobs needed more hands to harvest, spring planting, raising a barn, and such things. But these workers kept themselves clean and lived in tidy, if rather small, old homes. Most everyone knew everyone else in Hilltop and hardly anyone made any trouble.

But here, I saw people who hardly looked human—dirty and their clothes tattered. It made me very sad. However, children ran around yelling and laughing playing the games kids played no matter what was going on around them. But the adults really worried me. Would they see us as people to attack or beg for money or food or something?

Though we felt a lot of eyes on us, no one did anything. But as we left that sad little village at the edge of Portville, I heard grumbling in a threatening tone. I couldn't make out what they said, but I sure hope it wasn't something about telling people at the barn about us. I picked up the pace. Our time could even be shorter than I feared.

My three young companions led the way to the Big Barn since they knew this place far better than me.

There was a narrow passageway at the corner of two massive barn walls. Several yards to our left was the warehouse where the dragon trains unloaded. The sound of the waves crashing on the shore behind us covered the noise we made as we squeezed in between logs, broken lumber, sections of corral fencing and other odds and ends.

The light was even dimmer inside the barn than it was outside in the pre-dawn. Only a few oil lamps hung on long ropes over our heads. I recognized the long, wide aisles between dragon corrals and the tall columns that reached from the floor to the high ceiling. The odor of animal bodies and human sweat hung heavy in the muggy air. It was impossible to see anything clearly toward the far walls.

"It's all right," Altan whispered. "Everything looks much the same. Fitzwater, where would they put a troublesome dragon?"

"I would think close to the warehouse entrance next door where the trains are unloaded. That way, there are many pairs of eyes going to and fro to watch the young blue."

"I agree," said Mamun. "When I loaded pallets and wagons from the unloading dock to move to other storage areas, they would sometimes have a troublemaker tied down with his mouth muzzled to keep him still and quiet. Someone the size of Caerulus would be different. They put big dragons in one of the huts outside made of big wooden poles with no roof. The misery of the hot sun, cold wind, and such things kept the dragon worn out. A lot of them died out there. Or they calmed down and learned their lesson."

"So how do we get that close to the unloading dock?" I asked.

Altan looked around. "Ah, there," he pointed up front near the passageway to the warehouse where there was an empty pallet mounted with big heavy wheels. "Let's all push that big boy up front to the warehouse side as if we're going to off-load the next train." He turned to me. "You need to keep your face down in your chest because someone might recognize you. The three of us will do the same. A few will recognize us, but they might not realize we have been long gone."

"But what if someone knows good and well you all left with the escaping blue dragons?"

"I'll see them before they see me, but Mamun and Fitzwater, you both watch out, too, in case I miss a familiar face who would betray us. Believe it or not, Jaiden, there are some here who probably cheered our quick exit back then and wished they could have tagged along. I'll know who those are."

"All right. But what do we do when we find Baldric?"

"Let's just see where he is and how well he's tied down," Altan said. "Then we can plan something. We'll probably have to put our backs into moving one or two loads to show we're just four more lunkheads doing a man's job."

We headed for the pallet. The closer we got, the more the traffic increased as we weaved our way past a few guys running up and down the wide dirt aisles. We passed many stalls with one, two, and more dragons, including a few blue dragon families. It all brought back the fear I felt the last time I was here looking for Caerulus and the youngsters and then escaping, hoping we wouldn't get stopped.

When we reached the passage to the warehouse, my heart nearly jumped out of my chest as we wheeled the pallet toward the unloading dock.

Of course, the most I saw was along the edge of my vision because I only stared at the floor as I tagged along pushing the back end of the pallet.

Abruptly, Altan spoke. "Hold. The loading dock door is only half open. A train will be here soon, but not yet. Let's go slow. So far, it's not too crowded this morning. It was good we came so early. The last load was probably hours ago from a midnight train or two."

I never even thought about a dragon train traveling in the middle of the night, but then this is the big city!

"There," Fitzwater said. "I see a dragon tied down just like I said. It's a blue. But I can't tell if it's just hunched over or it's a younger, smaller one."

Altan said, "Wait here. I'll go up there. The guy at the receiving desk isn't familiar to me, so he shouldn't recognize me as a troublemaker."

He slowly approached the tight little corral. I didn't dare raise my face too much, yet I had to look. No such luck, I couldn't see enough to be sure.

Altan trotted back quickly. "I think it's Baldric. He fits your description perfectly, Jaiden."

"Good," I said, but I didn't mean it. At least not completely. I was glad we found him but now how would we get the young guy out without killing him and us?"

We spent almost an hour wandering about and acting as if we were part of the workforce. An opportunity opened up when a dragon train pulled in outside the main entrance. The conductor came up to a guy not much older than Altan standing by the entrance at a raised desk top piled with papers.

"Where's the Head Receiver?" the conductor asked the guy.

"He's not here yet," he scoffed. "I think maybe he stayed a little too long last night at the Working Man's Pub."

"Aw Hades! When will he learn?" He looked around impatiently. "So, can you check our shipment?"

"That's what he told me to do, if he, uh, was a little late. I've helped him before, I know what's what."

"Yeah, well, you better. I've got less than eight hours before I have to turn around and head back out with a new load to the Deadly Plains. I don't know what our Dear Leader has in mind..." His voice trailed off as if he had already said too much. But the young assistant didn't even look up.

The conductor handed a thick wad of papers to the assistant who took them and riffled through the pages as unloading crews began passing through the wide entrance from the dock. Crews from all over the barn came toward us to begin taking the materials to various areas designated for food, military equipment, clothing, and all manner of things an army needed.

"This is perfect," I said. "While they deal with this big shipment, we can blend in carrying loads and pass by the holding pen where the blue dragon rests. I'll reach out to him with my thoughts and let him know I am here with help and his father and mother aren't far away. Let's get busy."

We loaded up the goods left on the dock's edge. I didn't know much about such a job, but it was easy to follow the other guys' lead. They hoisted heavy boxes, stacking them so they were secure and allowed way more than I thought could be loaded on one pallet.

We purposely headed for the holding pen. As I passed, I focused on a simple message. 'Baldric, is that you? This is Jaiden. I'm with these guys pushing this load. Don't look at me or act like you hear me.'

I glanced at the blue form in the pen. His head began to raise, but he stopped himself from looking right at me. He seemed to focus on a pile of hay in front of him. *I hear you! Jaiden! I was so scared you wouldn't come back! Don't get in trouble. I'm all right for now, but there are men who come and talk about moving me. Taking me on a dragon train to some place. I don't like the sound of it and I don't know what they have in mind.*

'We're going to get you out now. But we have to figure out exactly how. Stay still, act like you don't care what's going on around you. Pretend to sleep, but don't actually sleep. When we have a plan, you have to be ready to run as soon as we get you loose.'

I'll be ready.

Over an hour passed as we hustled tons of materials off the dragon train. As we hauled it off to various areas located in the far corners of the warehouse, we whispered back and forth. After arguing a bit and straining our brains between the four of us, we came up with a plan. We had to do something unpredictable. I feared everyone was on guard for a rescue effort. In any case, now it was time to do it! As soon as word of the battle in the hills north of Lynden reached here, Baldric would either be killed or they would really be ready to stop a rescue effort. Or both.

Several stacks of supplies off the train stood waiting for us to keep loading. We placed the heaviest items on our pallet so it would be hard for these other men to move. We struggled to get it rolling and stopped near Baldric. I looked all around. No one was close.

'This is the time, Baldric. I will come into your pen and release your ropes. Stay still and don't act like anything is going on. I'll stay low so the people around can't see me. If you see anyone coming near, let me know so I can hide underneath you or get out of here. This may take a while.'

All right. I'll watch for anyone coming around.

I motioned for Fitzwater to help me with the ropes since he was bigger and stronger than the rest of us. We were making progress when someone came through the wide entrance. The way he moved with confidence and headed directly for the raised desk top, I could tell it was the Head Receiver. There was something familiar about him.

It was Meremoth! He was the stall boy my three friends didn't trust when I first came to the Big Barn. He was much bigger than before and had a look about him that made it clear he was in charge as he sat behind the raised desk top and shuffled papers.

"I don't believe it," Altan whispered hoarsely. "How did he move up in the world?"

"I don't care right now," I whispered back. "All I care about is getting Baldric out of here."

"Let me take care of this," Fitzwater offered, his blue eyes dancing. "I kicked his butt a couple of times when he was messing around not doing his work right and now it's time to cut him back down to size again."

Fitzwater tucked the end of a rope into his waistband and slowly approached Meremoth, who had his back to us. We worked feverishly getting the last of Baldric's ropes untied and put aside.

'Baldric,' I said in my mind. 'Slowly move toward us. We left a big space in the middle where you can fit between the wooden boxes.'

Mamun led the dragon between the boxes while Altan and I pushed him so he'd fit in the small space. Altan looked behind him.

"Fitzwater got Meremoth's attention. I don't think the butt-kissing *Head* Receiver has recognized him yet. Fitzwater's grown a lot in the last couple of years, too," he sniggered.

Just as we moved the boxes back together, Meremoth suddenly hit Fitzwater with a mace he pulled out from a drawer under his desktop. He cried out, "Attack! Attack! Dragon lovers are trying to take the blue punk! Attack!"

Like ants flying out of multiple holes in the ground in the wake of a brushfire, men came out of the dimness of the warehouse and even the Big Barn next door from all directions. Where did they come from? They were ready just as I feared. A couple of minutes before when I scanned the surrounding area, I saw the other crews in the far corners of the Barn and warehouse. Now they were just a few feet away as they rushed us brandishing maces, whips, and short chains.

What's happening! Baldric's frantic voice screamed in my head.

'Never mind,' I told him. 'Things are getting interesting. Stay put and don't make a sound!'

There was nothing at hand for the other guys to pick up to defend themselves except the ropes that had held Baldric in the pen. I pulled my slingshot out of my pouch and whirled it over my head since there was no room to spin it at my side. I slung a rock at the face of the biggest guy running toward us. He grabbed his face and yelped in pain.

Out of the corner of my eye, I saw Fitzwater regain his footing and grab one end of the rope from his waistband. He let out a length of about five feet and, like I did with my slingshot, he whirled it in a mad circle ready to whack anyone coming near. Altan and Mamun both grasped posts that held the railings of the pen together, ripped them away from the fencing, and prepared to swing them at any heads that came close.

Instinctively, I turned my back on Altan and Mamun as they did the same to me. The three of us kept the attacking men at bay. For a while. Facing the wide entrance where more young men rushed toward us, I saw Fitzwater throw down the rope and punch Meremoth in the face as he began working his way through the crowd between him and us, knocking them right and left with his bare fists.

Our brave and strong response slowed the approaching men. But we were so outnumbered and ill-equipped that it wouldn't take long for us to end up smashed to a pulp on the hay in Baldric's pen.

Then a roar, sounding like the battle cry of Hellmuth shook the heavy air of the Big Barn. I whipped my face to the far north end where the whirlwind of sound came from and saw Skye and Caerulus *galloping* toward us. They roared and screeched nearly making my ears bleed.

The crowd flooding in on us stopped in their tracks and as one, all turned their heads toward the attacking dragons. Within another moment, the blue mates were only twenty feet away from us when I saw them spread their wings just wide enough to glide over the floor without hitting the tall wooden columns supporting the roof. Then they clicked their back teeth together.

"Hit the floor you guys!" I cried out to my companions. "They're going to ignite their fire!"

"What?" I heard several of our attackers say. One tall, loud guy near me called out to the others. "They can't spew fire, they're train dragons and they can't—"

At that moment, I saw the pointed ends of the dragons' flames spew out. I ducked my head and buried my face in the smelly hay, hoping my companions did the same.

The heat of Skye and Caerulus' flames washed over us like a vicious whirlwind. I screamed as my back blistered but I kept my face down. The cavernous space of the Barn echoed with screams, shrieks, and bawling that sounded like babies in extreme pain. I heard the rush of the flames.

Barely raising my head, I tracked the two dragons as they circled us in opposite directions carefully dipping or raising their wing tips to avoid crashing into the wooden columns.

A rumble of feet stamping the dirt floor receded away from us. The heat decreased and blessed cool air descended on my body. I quickly scanned my hands and arms. They were red but not really burned. I looked around at Altan and Mamun. They were in a similar red, but not scalded, state. Altan lifted Mamun up on his feet and rushed to help me up, too.

"Are you all right? It looked like we were going to be barbequed like calves on a spit! Man, those dragons can really cook." Altan laughed. "They burned me, too, but nothing like all these poor guys around us."

I stood and saw men lying everywhere with blackened skin covering their bodies. Some moaned, a few cried, but most were still and silent.

"Great Creator and Hades below," I said. "They flash fried these guys on the run."

The two dragons circled us once more and then landed, each on either side of us.

"Baldric!" I yelled and turned to where we hid him. The boxes were black with soot and some spots smoldered with small flames and smoke.

After a long moment while I held my breath, a blue head popped up.

Mom, Dad! Am I glad to see you two! he called out, sounding more like the little guy I first met right here in this very barn. The big blues made that odd, snarking sound that was dragon laughter and moved toward Baldric as the three of us scrambled to get out of their way before they crushed us underfoot.

But relief was short. Coming in from the same far corner of the Big Barn was a silver streak flying low, weaving in an evasive pattern as his voice cut right into our brains, *Cannons! Cannons! The humans are rolling train cars this way with mounted cannons.*

I whipped my head right and left. Where was Fitzwater? Yet we had no time to waste. We had to make a quick getaway.

TWENTY-ONE

Cannon Fodder

Trigger coasted to a hard landing near us. He took in the scene of burned remains of the Big Barn crew, squinted his eyes, set his jaw and got down to business immediately. *Waste no time! Must leave now or cannons kill us. Fly out big door now.*

With his snout, the silver pointed out the wide where the train dragons entered and left the barn. The train that had unloaded earlier was now gone so we had a clear exit but how long before the cannons block our way?

I turned to Caerulus. "What do we do? You've seen the cannons in action."

The human boys need to get on Skye and hang on. Your lives depend on it. No time to use ropes or leather straps. Caerulus motioned with his head toward the way out. *Look and you will see the roof that extends outside the entrance. We have to clear that before we can fly up out of range of the cannons. So we can either fly slow but zig-zag sharply so the cannons can't get us in their sights or we fly fast in a straight line to the west and then up and travel beyond the edge of the city.*

I turned to the guys and explained the choices.

Altan spoke up immediately, "I think I would get too dizzy darting back and forth. I'd rather hang on and hope I don't get blown off."

"Yeah, me too," Mamun said.

"But what about Fitzwater?" I cried. The two boys' eyes widened as they looked at each other.

"Hades! You're right," Altan spat the words out. "He's not here."

We looked out across the mass of burned bodies. Some people still moaned in pain while others lay as still as rocks. In spite of what they tried to do to us, I felt bad about the pain they suffered. But more importantly, Fitzwater was nowhere in sight.

"Do you think he got away?" Mamun asked.

"Or was taken prisoner before the dragons came in?" Altan added.

I looked at my feet and my hands, red from the dragons' flames. "The last I saw, he was punching and wading his way towards me through a big bunch of men. But then—it was all so confusing..

Enough! Caerulus cut into my mind while his voice roared out loud. All three of us were jerked back to our own present danger. *It is admirable you want to find him, whether dead or alive, but we have no time for such luxuries. We go now. Look for him later.*

"Caerulus says we don't have time."

"Of course," Altan said. "He's right but we can't leave him." He avoided looking me in the eye. "I don't know what to do... as much as it hurts to leave our friend. If we could only find him—never mind, let's go or none of us will get out of here alive. We fly straight out of here, no darting around." Altan's gaze bored into me.

I honestly would have preferred zigzagging, but maybe that was because I was used to flight on the back of a dragon, especially after flying on crazy Trigger. I saw their point, so I nodded in agreement. "Let's fly, guys," I said.

Baldric interrupted, *I can fly on my own. No need to carry me like a baby—*

You'll do no such thing, his mother said so strongly, it startled me, too. *You can't fly like either of us yet, but your time is coming, just not today. Get on your father.* She turned to me and said, *Tell Altan to get on me. Have Mamun get on Caerulus because with Baldric to carry, he'll need as light a load as he can get.*

"All right, but I'll go on Trigger while Altan and Mamun ride on you, Skye, making it even better for Baldric going on Caerulus."

"What?" Altan said.

"Sorry, but we're talking in our minds. No arguments! Both of you get on Skye and hang on as tight as you possibly can."

"Yeah, well, we're going to take just a moment." Altan grabbed a handful of partly burned ropes that had tied Baldric down. He quickly pulled two lengths of rope and handed one to Mamun and took the other for himself. He reached down for another and offered it to me.

"No, that's all right," I said. "The leather straps I use to ride Trigger will work just fine. I left them on him just in case things got out of hand. And things are definitely out of all our hands..." I looked over at the three dragons " And claws, too. Right?"

Right. Now let's get out of here. Caerulus insisted. *I refuse to let us become so much cannon fodder for these beastly humans!*

In the quick moves of guys who knew a thing or two about securing loads, the two boys wrapped their ropes around Skye's middle and climbed on. Baldric, like he had done for years as a youngster, latched onto his father's spines. Trigger grunted impatiently as I mounted up.

Caerulus roared. *Let's fly, dragons. West and then north as fast as you can flap your wings!*

Caerulus reached to the rafters with his long wings and pulled them back and down, blowing debris from our battle backwards in a flurry like a high wind. He lifted and sailed to the left through the wide entrance into the morning light.

A loud boom like thunder shook the Big Barn and made the dirt floor vibrate and shift as if it were turning into quicksand. A ball of fire flew past the wide doorway just after Caerulus' tail disappeared upwards.

Skye reached more forward with the tips of her wings and drew them back to stir up the battle debris that hadn't settled from her mate's liftoff. She glided swiftly to the right and flew low over the dock. She then turned and dropped lower, disappearing from view.

Another boom rattled the Big Barn as a second ball of fire flew by in a high line, but Skye was already gone.

"What's going to happen to us?" My heart pounded hard against my ribs. This might be the last few moments of our young lives. I dug into Trigger's ribs with my knees.

Trigger turned back to me and gave me that same smart aleck grin he did just before our first ride. Oh, this should be good, I thought and braced myself for a rip-roaring launch.

We flew out of the Big Barn like a bolt launched from a double-strung crossbow. I didn't think I had the strength to hang on. But I guess the tight wrap and the tough leather held me tightly while my arms felt like they were going to part ways from my shoulders.

We soared into light so bright it cut through my eyes like knives. I glanced to my right to see two trains, *not* towed by dragons but pushed by gangs of soldiers, coming toward us along the side of the Barn. Both had massive iron cannons mounted on flat cars aimed right at us. I heard a loud bellow from a big man standing on a small platform attached to the front of one of the train cars just to the side of the cannon.

"Fire!" The big man roared.

The cannon nearest him belched fire that spewed out in a thin sheet of sparks followed by something black and round racing through the sparks toward us.

"Faster!" I screamed and tightened my grip, almost disjointing my knuckles.

Trigger dipped downward so fast, the scalp on my head strained to separate from the rest of my skull. I felt a horrifying heat spread over my body as the fireball flew behind us.

He spun right and we came up on the side of the cannon car before he banked left over a scattering of low buildings.

Missed us! Barely.

As we flew over rickety buildings thrown together with all manner of rough lumber, I caught a heavy scent of wet leather and manure—dragons. Lots of dragons. I looked down into a large corral and saw very old and very young dragons milling around as they looked up at us, mouths wide open in shock.

Trigger mumbled, *The old and the frail. Worn-out work dragons and youngsters of those taken away in forced labor. They are starving to death. Cheaper than killing. Those too weak are fed to guard dogs and other animals the humans keep. I pulled carts loaded with their dying bodies. A disgusting job humans forced me to do before I escaped.*

"Great Creator, how horrible. I don't think Hades is hot enough for the likes of those who have done this to dragons and the other poor beasts these humans use. The worst people in my village would never stoop so low to treat any living thing this bad. Is there anything we can do to help?"

You want to die now? We can't help them.

"Go down anyway, it'll only take a moment."

Trigger shuddered but didn't talk back to me. We dove down so fast, I almost lost my breakfast. No time to throw up, so I swallowed hard, ran over to the corral gate and struggled to open it. Trigger followed me and grabbed the rope holding it closed. He jerked it open.

There, that's all we can do. Now, we're gone, my rider. Hang on, I haven't yet stretched my wings enough to give you a really good ride!

I swung on and he took off while I struggled to tighten the straps. I heard more loud booms and angry yelling behind us but they faded quickly. I hoped in the confusion of our escape, that some of the captive dragons could escape. It was probably stupid of me, but at least I did something.

The wind roared in my ears as we sped up and gained altitude. My ears popped and my weary hands, arms and shoulders struggled to hang on. Ahead, I saw two massive pairs of wings pull the blue dragons and their precious cargo higher and faster. The feisty silver dragon pulled hard on his wings to bring us close behind the blue pair.

Caerulus was right. He, along with Skye and Trigger made sure none of us were going to end up cannon fodder.

The air chilled me to the bone but the freedom in my heart made it all worthwhile.

TWENTY-TWO

Storm Approaches

Since our return to Septrion, I spent the best part of two days sleeping and eating but not much else. I don't know why battles left me exhausted. First, after the ambush of Ubel's army and then again after Baldric's rescue. Skye also had Altan and Mamun stay here with me though they didn't spend much time with me.

They were getting around, with Jarmil's help, to meet the other dragons in the Novis' village.

Caerulus had flown back and forth twice to meet with Hellmuth and others of the High Council at the Founders' village. The morning of the third day was the last day of peace in Septrion and the surrounding desert. Enough time had passed for the Army of the Dear Leader and the Dragon Train Army to be on their way to Lynden. We had every reason to expect the worst.

Silvers under Skye's command flew over the region around Lynden. They also carefully surveyed the foothills of the northern Emerald Forest watching for dragon trains filled with soldiers and equipment, especially those fearsome cannons. Of course, there could already be small battalions sneaking through the forest as an early strike force before larger forces and heavy weapons made their way north.

Caerulus dropped in early the third day. His sons and daughter clustered around him. *I don't have much time, but I want to be sure the young ones are still all right.*

"No problem," I said. "Baldric, here, is quite the hero and tells his story constantly. I think Deryn and Jarmil have even shared their story with some of the other young dragons in Novis. Don't be surprised if a few of those dragons want to follow you around. Same thing for Altan and Mamun, but I think they kind of like the attention. As for me... Well I don't let them get away with making me out the big hero because I'm not—"

Of course you are, he insisted, surprising me. *We couldn't have done it without you and the boys sneaking into the Big Barn... But don't think you're some kind of special... whatever. We don't have time for pride to cloud our thinking.*

I sensed an edge in the way he said that. Funny, how I was starting to really sense his and Skye's emotions through those "head voices."

I hoped he wasn't going to tell me off, but at that moment, thank the Creator, Skye came in to spend time with the children.

"How goes it out there?" I asked, relieved that Caerulus didn't have a chance to say any more.

What? She looked at me then Caerulus with her mouth open as if she was going to say something out loud, but then stopped herself. *Oh, you mean about the angry humans coming our way.* She took a deep breath and hunkered down on her customary stone bench facing her mate, children and me. *I assure each of you everything is being done to protect our northern lands from direct attack.*

Mother, Baldric said. *I now know what's at stake and though I'm not full grown, I feel like I am after what I went through. I am grateful for all that you, Father, Jaiden and his friends did to rescue me. I should do something more and not just be left here with the children—*

Hey, Deryn interrupted. *I'm not a child! I'm only a little younger than you. It's Jarmil that's the child.*

Jarmil made a little squawking sound. *No, I'm not! I'll box those nasty humans in the face if they get near me again!*

Children, children, Sky insisted. *It is our duty to protect you most of all. There will be a time for all three of you to take your place among the adult blue dragons...* Her voice in my head drifted off into what I recognized as dragon language. But I could sense her tension.

Caerulus, on the other hand, roared in frustration. *Quiet, all of you! Even I don't know what war will really be like, but I know how I felt these last few days. And when I talk with Hellmuth and the other leaders... Never mind.* He roared again, shaking down loose pieces of the cave ceiling on our heads.

As soon as he let loose with his vocal outburst, he spun around, paced toward the cave entrance, stopped and turned slowly to face us. His breathing became labored and his mouth his eyes were downcast. *It's not you I'm mad at. These humans will never give up until we defeat them so severely, they can't recover their forces. And I'm not sure we can do that. We have to come up with every means to defend and to attack surpassing our traditional battle methods. After all, we lost the Dragon Wars...*

The cave was very quiet after that for several moments. Then I said, "Tell you what, let me see what I can hunt up for a nice supper so we can all just settle down and let our heads clear."

Good idea, Jaiden, Sky said. *Don't you think so, my brave mate?*

Caerulus actually nodded his head and moved over to his children and hunkered down near them without a word. The youngsters seemed to understand and calmed down. I made a quick exit before I said anything stupid to ruin the moment.

During the following day, Baldric regaled his sister and brother again with stories of how he resisted and frustrated his human captors. I was still tired from the experience and a little embarrassed when he brought me up in his tales.

Our beloved friend, Jaiden, Baldric said, *and his friends from the Big Barn, fought bravely and devastated the nasty humans who held me for all those days.* He launched into a lively retelling of his grand adventure. *You don't remember the three boys, Altan, Mamun, and Fitzwater, but for the second time, they risked their lives along with Jaiden to get me loose and on Father's back. Because of them we flew out with our tails nearly burning from the balls of fire the humans' evil cannons threw at us. Poor Fitzwater, we just don't know what happened to him but Jaiden said they would go back to find him. Anyway, the humans couldn't touch us with their mighty fire and iron!*

On second thought it was good to be the hero of Baldric's high tales of adventure. After his story, Deryn, came over to me and gave me a bashful dragon smile. At least, that's what it looked like. Then she said the darnedest thing. *Jaiden, I'm very proud of you... and grateful, too. You saved Jarmil and me from everything that Baldric went through.*

Deryn wasn't as big as Baldric, but she could raise her face to look me right in the eye. The silver flecks in her eyes danced around her pupils that suddenly opened really wide like she had just seen something shocking.

"Is something the matter?" I asked.

She dropped her eyelids and looked at my feet. *No, nothing's the matter.* She took a deep breath and then raised her head back up and met my eyes with an intense stare. It made me feel like she was peering right into my soul. *I didn't know it was you until just now. You were so young when—Sorry! I don't know what I'm saying. I'm just now realizing who I—*

She dropped her gaze again and slowly swung her head side to side. Like she was looking for an escape route.

"Uh... I don't know what you're trying to say," I said to her as she looked away from me. "You must still be upset about all that's happened. It was scary when they tried to take us captive in Lynden. I'm really glad your mother was able to rescue—"

No that's not it. Deryn turned and looked up at me, smiling shyly. *I'm just a child who hasn't gotten her head together yet. Glad you're back. Thanks, bye.*

She moved away about as fast as a young dragon could go.

Her little performance stunned me. What was *that* about? Are young dragon girls just as silly as human girls? Maybe sillier? Boys are usually stupid, I should know. But girls are all emotions and silliness. I kind of like that about girls, but then Wyetta... she was something else. And I hadn't figured that out, either.

Fortunately, I didn't have time to dwell on silly girls and stupid boys because Skye came over and gave me a look. "What?" I said. "Are you reading my mind again?"

I don't need to when it's all over your face. What did Deryn say to you that has you confused?

"I don't have a clue what she was getting at. Just silly girl stuff, I guess. Anyway, I'm glad you came over, it was getting embarrassing. I think your daughter was trying to thank me for saving her and Jarmil but it came out all weird."

I felt better right away. Skye had that effect on me. Everything was more real when I talked with her. I knew she had met Wyetta after we returned from Portville, so my guess was that she had something to say about her. I was right.

I saw your girlfriend yesterday when I stopped by Luc and Owyn's cave and... I found her... she's not exactly—

"Whatever you think about her, she's not my girlfriend! She's way too pretty to be interested in the likes of me. And she's a real tough warrior. She did better than I did when the fight broke out when you ambushed the dragon train soldiers bringing us north out of Lynden. Besides, she's a little older than me. I'm just a kid to her," I said rather disappointed at the truth of the matter.

Don't degrade yourself like that. If she would have seen you and your friends rescue Baldric—

"Yeah, well, she didn't. And I'm not going to brag on myself because I'm my father's son. And that isn't what we do. My dad never bragged about himself and, like it or not, I'm the same way. So I'm not going to think or say any different about myself."

So now you're quoting the wisdom of your father, she said with a devilish dragon smile on her face.

"I know, crazy, huh? Still, she's not my girlfriend, but I hope she considers herself a friend after what we went through together."

Skye sighed. *All right, I won't try to be your mother in this, but I... I'm sorry but I don't quite know what to make of her. I'm not an expert on human women, but she will have to prove herself more to me before I feel she can be a*

*good friend to you. I just want you to be careful. That's all
I'm going to say about her.*

"Thanks. Your feelings are noted. You've become much
more than a friend to me. We have flown together and
shared so much good and not a little danger in the last few
weeks besides our adventures two years ago. You're like...
Uh, more than a friend."

I got lost in the confusing feelings and words all racing
through my head, so I couldn't express myself. What was
Skye to me? I had no one in all my life like her. My dad
was—my dad. He brought me into this world through my
mother, but he was hardly ever close to me. He had a lot of
anger that he sent my way. I sort of understood, but I
wished he had been more like some of my friend's fathers.
But then, without him, I would be nothing. Literally.

Yet, Skye... she was the biggest thing in my life. A place
of comfort and understanding... I think. I laughed to
myself. She was the largest living thing I knew, except for
Caerulus and scary old Hellmuth, but she was so much
bigger in my life. I just couldn't put words to it, so I'll just
leave it at that.

*There's something else you'll find out about soon
enough. There are small groups of humans heading into
the Septrion. Not enemies or soldiers of the Dear Leader
or the Dragon Train company, but free people who want to
join our cause.*

"Really? I'm amazed."

*Me, too, but Hellmuth, Caerulus, and others are
suspicious so we are confining the friendly humans to a
small valley west of here. Safe from any attack from
Lynden, yet under our watch from both the Novis and the*

Founders. You will be needed and, perhaps, your girl—no, your friend Wyetta to test their sincerity about joining our cause. Of course, we can't talk to them because they can't hear our thoughts like you can.

"I still don't understand why," I said.

Maybe someday we'll all understand that. What is more important is that in spite of their opinion about humans, both Hellmuth and my mate know human hands will be needed in this new war with humanity. In fact the two of you can talk to them—

"But what do we say? Do I let on I can communicate with you through our minds? I've not even told Wyetta that."

And that is how it must be for now. But you can act like you can understand us much like you would know your own farm animals. It's a little insulting to us, but we can't let even sympathetic humans know how we communicate with you.

"I will be very careful," I said, "and act like I'm sort of in charge here. But don't let Hellmuth come around too soon because it'll be obvious that no one in charge of him."

Good. And there's something else. Owyn and Luc brought word to me as soon as the first people arrived that there was one young woman, a girl really, among them who talked to them as if she believed they could understand and gave your name as a close friend of hers from Hilltop. The two brothers were upset that somehow she knew about how we communicate, but then after a while, she also went around to anyone who would listen to her, saying the same thing over and over.

"Really? Who would that be?" I couldn't imagine or think of anyone who would say that.

She said her name was Aleena—

"Aleena! My Creator, she's this, this little *girl*. Well, a little more than a little girl, but not much of a friend. Much younger than me, I barely know her." I ran out of air and stupid things to say.

Nevertheless, she kept saying over and over again that she knew you and you would vouch for her. She didn't promise to be a great warrior but she wants to help for the good of Hilltop. I came around her so I could overhear it for myself. As I watched her, I could tell by the way her face brightened when she spoke of you with a tremble in her voice that she admires you greatly.

Who in the world would have thought that little mousy girl... Oh dad-blamed it! I recalled her little greeting to me after she snuck up on me months ago, before I left Hilltop with Skye to come here. I didn't think she was serious, but there you are. Somehow that daughter of Alden left Hilltop and joined up with other people coming here before she got lost or starved to death.

Crazy! Never mind. It was something to think about for another day. Not that I was much interested in her before, but I was very curious about this so-called admiration of me that brought her here. Of all places and times!

It was early evening. I needed to clear my head of so much confusion about Skye and what she really meant to me, the dangerous times we lived in, this girl, this Aleena of all people, silly little Deryn... and then there was Wyetta, beautiful and capable. It was too much to think about.

I walked out to the big stone benches, where the dragons often reclined near their cave, and looked across the desert valley. Dozens of mesas, some shaped like ghosts and hoodoos, still glowed softly in the orange sunset. My shadow extended a hundred yards toward the east joining the scattered mesas as if I was a pinnacle of sandstone among similar shapes.

Skye came up behind me. I turned and saw the strangest thing. She had something in her mouth. She leaned down near me, dropped the object she held and gazed deep within me with those copper-flecked eyes.

I found something for you. This was among the scattered weapons after the battle with Ubel's soldiers on the big hill. You had already fainted and that girl— Wyetta—and Trigger carried you off to Azure Den. I knew this was something you had wanted for some time. Tell me what you think.

I looked down at my feet. It was a crossbow. Beautifully formed of ash and yew glued together to form the bow, the best woods for a crossbow! Its graceful curves, the finely crafted metal parts—the pawl that held the bowstrings until released by the trigger—all enthralled me to my core. It was amazing. A long thick leather bag held more than a dozen sharp bolts the length of my forearm.

I had only seen a crossbow this fine once before when a rich farmer who lived nearby showed it to my father. Of course my dad acted like he wasn't impressed. But I couldn't forget it. The burning desire for one of my own was lit from then on.

"For me?" I said with a squeak in my voice like I was a twelve-year-old. "But you—Caerulus said I wasn't ready and that neither of you could train me—"

We will figure it out together. And, you'll never guess. Old Tristram knows a thing or two about such things. I had a brief talk with Hellmuth when I went with Caerulus to meet with the High Council of the Founders when we first got back from Portville. Hellmuth knew Tristram from the Dragon Wars. He was a brave human soldier who saw the horror of war between people and us. He turned out to be very useful to us. He knew your mother and father—

"Yeah, he told me that when our cells were next to each other in the prison. I'll be darned, no... I'll be *gol*-durned! So, he was telling the truth! I thought he was playing games with me but I came to trust him in spite of my suspicions. So he is a friend of dragons and—everything he said is true!"

Anyway, the point is, he should be able to train you to use a crossbow. He may not be known as one of the best among crossbow arbalists—that's an expert with a crossbow—but he will do.

"Does that mean Tristram is feeling better now?" I asked, dreading the possible answer.

Yes, I was called to Luc and Owyn's when we returned with our children. He's doing much better and got very excited to hear how well you and the boys did helping us rescue Baldric. He'll be up and about in no time.

Skye paused and looked far to the east. I could tell by her gaze that she was seeing something well beyond the mesas as they dimmed in the last light of day.

And another thing. Hellmuth spoke often of a storm approaching. Not a weather storm, but a storm of battle, killing, raids...

"War," I said, unable to cover up my sadness. "The Dragon Wars aren't over after all. But what will it be like this time?"

It will be beyond our imagination. What we experienced from those cannons when we escaped the Big Barn—that's only a small sample. A little fire in a big pit. What is to come will be a firestorm that will cover this desert around us, and the trees, villages, and people of the Emerald Forest, the Nulland Plains, the Deadly Plains to the west, and all along the eastern coast to Portville into the very Capitol of the humans' Dear Leader.

I could hardly draw a breath. "All of us. You, your mate, your children, the dragons—Novis and Founders, my father, all the people of the forests and plains. None will be spared, will they?"

I'm afraid not, she said simply.

We both walked to the edge of the cliff that dropped several hundred feet to a rugged valley. Beyond lay the plains covered with mesas as far as my eyes could see. I swung the crossbow up, a little put off by its weight and yet thrilled by the power contained in the relaxed bowstrings and wood of its bow. But when I learned to pull those strings and hook them, loaded a bolt and took aim... that would be when I truly became a man. Or so I thought.

I looked up at Skye as she enclosed me within the span of her beautiful blue wings protecting and inspiring me to face the approaching storm.

End Book 2

Next...

Dragon Train War

RJ enjoys writing fantastical stories of all sorts, including Dragon Train tales, along with music, volunteering and adventure.

RJ and his wife spend a lot of time with Trixie–their famous rescue dog–as well as family and friends.

CPSIA information can be obtained
at www.ICGtesting.com
Printed in the USA
BVHW081907231222
654914BV00002B/199